SCARS OF

August

THE AUGUST SERIES

ASHLEY PIERCE

*To anyone who's ever loved someone so completely that you
forgot to love yourself, this one's for you.*

PROLOGUE

May 16th 2009

It's the perfect day—seventy degrees with a light breeze and not a cloud in the sky.

But I'm sweating, and my hands are clammy. I don't know why. We've done this before. Yet something about this whole morning has had my stomach heavy and a looming feeling in the air that today is different somehow.

This suit, which I've worn a handful of times before, suddenly feels suffocating. The material is the worst thing I've ever felt on my skin. I swallow a bundle of nerves, which reminds me that this tie is probably a little too tight. I wish I could rip it off. Her dad has already had to help me fix it. *Twice.*

We sit together familiarly on the couch, talking about various things, just as we normally would. Today is not–should not–be anything other than a normal day at my best friend's house. I'm sitting on the same couch I've sat on since we were kids, waiting for her to come into the room. I've done this hundreds of times. My fingers pick at the hard plastic seam of the box sitting at my side. The noise adds a cadence in the background like a clock ticking. I hope it's distracting, but I think it's done the opposite.

"I don't need to lecture you tonight, do I?" her dad asks.

A nervous laugh slips through my lips. Does he? "No, sir," I say, immediately regretting my word choice. I've never called him that before. *Why would I now?* He notices too.

"Oh?" his eyebrow arches. "Because normally I'd lecture someone who comes over and anxiously fidgets while sitting on my couch and calls me sir."

"Sorry." I backpedal.

He lets out another low laugh. "No need. It's kind of funny to see you nervous like this."

So, it's not just me. Whatever I'm feeling is obvious enough to be called out on. Before I can lie and say I'm not, her mom runs into the room, camera in hand.

"Okay, they're ready! Are you?" she chirps.

He stands up, so I do the same. Not sure why, but my anxiety tells me to go with the flow.

"Okay!" her mom calls down the hall. "Come out!"

Within a couple of seconds, *she* rounds the corner, except for a brief moment, I question if it's actually her. As her eyes meet mine and she smiles, the doubt rushes away. She sparkles, and I'm not sure if it's from all the glitter on her dress or just her smile alone.

As the sound of her mom's camera clicks away, she walks towards me, and I remember I'm supposed to put this flower on her wrist.

"Hi." She says quietly.

"Hi," I say back, sounding as timid as I feel.

I really want to tell her she looks gorgeous, but I can't bring myself to form words, especially not with her parents hovering over me.

"Wait, before you do that, we have one more." Her mom says, just as her other best friend rounds the corner.

They're dressed in almost the same way, yet there's no comparison. My eyes go right back to her just as her head turns back to me. Her smile reappears, and we carry on to what we were doing.

Out of the corner of my eye, I can see her mom rush to get to a spot where her camera has a view. I take the bundle of flowers out of the plastic case and slide it onto her wrist. She grabs the matching rose bud and pins it to the lapel of my jacket as we share another silent smile before her mom ushers us outside.

"Let's get some of you guys before everyone else gets here." She directs us to the same spot in the yard she always has for pictures, then begins clicking away.

"How many of the same picture is too many?" I whisper against her head.

She laughs, looking up at me, and the sound of it replaces just a bit of nervousness with contentment, dare I say excitement? I would've never said no to her asking me to be her stand-in date, but now that we're here, I'm more than happy I agreed.

"The limit does not exist." She whispers, referencing one of her favorite movies—one I've had to sit through a million times. But that movie makes her laugh out loud every time she watches it, so I do it willingly.

"Put your hand on his chest so that I can see the matching flowers." Her mom directs again.

She does as she's told, and the action brings us closer together. I suck in a breath as my hand rests on her lower back.

"Oh, you kids are going to have the best night. No one ever forgets prom night."

I smile even though the statement doesn't ring true for me. My prom was last year, and honestly, nothing about it is worth remembering. But then I look down and see her eyes looking back up at me—bright, sparkling, and full of something that's not just excitement.

Suddenly, the nerves I've been fighting all day, combined with the feeling in my chest now, I'm starting to think that this prom night might actually be the one we'll remember.

CHAPTER ONE

Autumn - May 2019

The screech of packing tape sealing up the last box echoes in the empty room. I slide myself over to lean against the wall, relieved that this part is over.

Ten years ago, I moved to Wisconsin. Not quite across the world, but far enough away from my home in Michigan. I was eighteen years old with no solid plan. I had no idea if I'd move back after school, or if I'd stay here. As cliché as they come, I just knew that I needed to get out of my hometown, and college gave me the perfect escape route.

I surprised everyone by leaving, even my parents. They all assumed I'd go to one of the local colleges, like almost everyone else from our class planned to, including my closest friends. No one even knew I applied out of state, and when the acceptance letter came, it stayed quietly in my dresser drawer for six months.

I knew my parents would try to stop me, especially my mom. I'm an only child, and they had just settled their divorce. My dad was the one to move out, so my also leaving was the last thing she would want.

Not that my dad would miss me less, but he's quite different than my mom, very quiet, stoic, and serious. His emotions are locked tightly away in a safe, while my mom's are hanging on the hem of her sleeve. She is undoubtedly a lover and loves hard. If she didn't hug and kiss me at least twice a day, something was wrong.

I don't mean to make my dad sound like a jerk, because he isn't. He was a great dad, and I knew I was his little girl, without the constant shower of affection. When I was little, he played with me and did all the doting dad duties, but once I started 'coming of age,' I don't think he knew how to handle it, so he tagged my mom in the ring.

I've wondered if my mom's constant attention would have been different if I had siblings. I don't know if I was an only child on purpose, but I've never asked. I was always afraid of the answer because I could not see my mom not being open to more babies.

The differences in their personalities always intrigued me, and I also used to wonder if it ultimately caused their split.

There was never much PDA between them besides a quick kiss in passing. As a kid, I never thought twice, but as an adult, I can understand how that might not have worked for someone like my mom.

Given that they never fought in front of me, the real reason for their split also remains a mystery. One that I'm not sure even warrants an answer after all this time.

I was quiet about my plan to leave because my friends would try and talk me out of it, too. They all kept talking about how great it was going to be, how everyone would still be together, and how nothing would have to change, but that was exactly what I *didn't* want.

So, graduation came and went without a word about it. Once that was all over with, I finally told my parents. Obviously, they needed to know first. I knew I would need their help with dorm stuff and moving.

The next person I told was Kory, my closest girlfriend. She was disappointed but didn't fight me too much because she knew why I wanted to go. We spent most of that summer with it as our little secret—all the way up to the week before move-in day.

When I finally told everyone else in our friend group, they were confused for a hot second, but quickly moved on to their upcoming plans and excitement for their own new chapters.

The only one who didn't immediately move on to the next topic of conversation was Jimmy, my other closest friend.

He asked me *'why?'* a hundred times, but I never told him the whole truth. Only that I wanted the whole college experience, including living on campus, it wasn't *not* the truth, just not the *full* truth.

The night before I left, he and Kory came over for dinner and to say goodbye. My dad came for the night, too, since we had to leave so early the next day.

I remember it being so awkward for my parents, but I hoped it would also be a good turning point. They were already getting along pretty well for that fresh, post-divorce stage, but I didn't think they had spent much time alone since separating, if any at all. I expected the sevenish-hour drive home after dropping me off to be interesting.

I was thankful for the dinner. We all sat around the table together talking, laughing, and ignoring the elephant in the room for as long as possible. Even though we were all trying to ignore it, I could see the confusion in Jimmy's face the whole time. He was acting like he was happy, but I could tell he wasn't. I also knew, well suspected, that he knew there was more to my leaving story, but he never said anything, and that only solidified my decision.

They stayed pretty late into the evening, much past dinner. My dad had to finally kick them out, unable to avoid saying, 'Four a.m. sure comes quick.'

Kory left first, teary-eyed and squeezing me to death. She made me promise a hundred times to call her every day. We wrapped our pinkies together, officially binding the promise, then she finally slumped into her car and drove away.

Jimmy had to wait for a ride since he didn't have a car at the time. That gave us time to be alone on the porch, which I wasn't sure if I wanted or not. All that accompanied us in those patio chairs was the August breeze and awkward silence; no words were spoken. I still don't understand why he didn't take that time to say anything. Ask anything. *Do* anything.

Eventually headlights pulled into the driveway, so we stood up and hugged. My stomach flipped, and I knew I would miss that. Something about his hugs was always my favorite. Finally, I felt sad and didn't want to let him go. My best friend since kindergarten, I couldn't remember life without him in it.

I tried to just soak it all in, but at the same time, not forgetting my plan and the reason behind it. I held onto him to absorb the memory. Even though I wanted to leave it all behind, I didn't want to forget what that felt like.

That time, it was *me* standing there, teary-eyed. While still imprinting the feeling of his hug, I told him I would miss him. He told me he'd miss me too. When his mom beeped the horn, I realized I didn't know how long we had been standing there like that. We stepped away from each other, and I remember that he looked just as sad as I felt.

"See you around, kid," he said with a glossy-eyed half smile.

I laughed like I always did when he called me 'kid.' He started that when he turned thirteen. Turning thirteen meant he was a teenager, but I was still only twelve, which meant I was still 'just a kid.' Even once I too became a teenager, he continued calling me that.

"Yeah." I told him, "See you around."

But I didn't. That was the last time we saw each other or even spoke.

And now, first thing in the morning, I'm going back. Thanks to social media, I know most of my old 'friends' never left, including Kory, Jimmy, and his now wife.

I really don't know what led me back. After finishing undergrad, I got this apartment, and at that time, I honestly never thought I'd leave. I was so happy here. With few distractions, I blew through nursing school and landed a great job right away.

Until about eight months ago, I would have said I was never leaving. I went back once, the first Christmas break after I left, but I had been *very* set on not ever going again. So, my parents came to see me for the majority of the holidays through the years. Yet one day, out of nowhere, homesickness finally set in and abruptly became overwhelming.

When I found myself emotional about everything relating to home and just wanting to be around my family again, I knew I wasn't going to last much longer.

Then the feelings got worse. Without my prompting, Kory sent me a job posting for an afternoon shift lead nurse at the hospital near home. I hadn't even told her about my nostalgic emotions yet; she just knew things like that somehow.

I applied instantly, and they called me the next day for an interview. By the end of the week, the job was mine, and I gave notice to my current boss and landlord.

I actually did both of those things before even talking to my mom to ask if I could stay with her. I knew she would say yes, though, that phone call was more me telling her I was coming home rather than asking. She was elated.

This living room now looks incredibly sterile. I wasn't allowed to paint, so I did everything I could to decorate the walls and bring some life into the place anyway. I forgot how unpleasant plain white walls looked until everything came down.

I stand up and do a walk-through for the millionth time to make sure nothing gets left behind. I see a few bobby pins sitting in the bathroom. As I pick them up, I notice my reflection in the mirror.

I've never been one for trends, so my sandy blonde hair has always been the same—long layers with full bangs. My forehead is far too big to ever go without them. I get a trim every two months to keep the length perfectly at my eyebrows.

My eyes, which occasionally change between a bright blue and light blue, are looking rather icy today. I love them when they are like this. With luck on my side, I haven't gained much weight since high school, still wearing some of my favorite shirts and hoodies.

After just spending the last few minutes strolling down memory lane, I stare at myself and shake my head at the irony of this whole situation. I left a decade ago because I didn't want things to stay the same. But here I am at twenty-eight, looking exactly the same as eighteen.

That thought leads me to the kitchen, where the pile of mail from yesterday is sitting. Adding to the irony is that in that pile is an invitation to our ten-year *'Homecoming'* high school reunion. *I couldn't make this stuff up if I tried.*

Details explained that due to many scheduling conflicts during the summer, they decided to do it in the fall, when a lot of people are home for the holidays. That led to the

'Homecoming Dance' theme, which also usually happens in the fall. I don't know if I care much about going, but I also know that if Kory went behind my back to give up my address, she would insist we go. *Kory.*

She really was and is my best friend. We kept that front porch promise and did, in fact, talk almost every day. I tried to make new friends here, but no one ever really stuck. Maybe I'm the problem, but meeting new people never really lived up to the hype.

We were in the fifth grade, both ten years old, when she came to our school. She was the new girl, but didn't act like it. She had the same outgoing personality back then that she does now, and fit right in. She made friends easily, and at first, that didn't even include me. Not for any reason in particular, she just hadn't made it to me yet.

Once we were assigned to be science fair partners, it was over. We spent a weekend together working on our experiment, which was *What Brand of Bubble Gum Blows the Biggest Bubble.* We laughed, chewed, blew, popped, chewed and blew again, picked sticky strings off our chins, and then laughed some more. Baseball gum blew the biggest, then Hubba Bubba in second place.

I don't remember a weekend after that when we didn't at least see each other on one of the days.

Kory was my person, and even with time and distance, that never changed. She's made a few trips to visit, and then once FaceTime became a thing, we were on it all the time. To this day, she knows everything there is to know about me, and I with her. She knows everything about everyone I've met here, the friends I tried to like, and the guys I tried to date, including the two that actually hurt.

Plus, she was the *only* one who had always known the full truth behind why I left, which meant she was the *only* one who knew why I was so nervous to come back.

CHAPTER TWO

Jimmy

The angry woman in front of the desk glares up at me.

"What do you mean there's nothing you can do?" she snarls, her face getting a brighter shade of red each time I repeat what she's already been told.

"We do not have connected rooms at this location." I calmly reply.

She huffs for the fifteenth time and tucks her hair behind her ears, preparing to also repeat herself. "When I booked, I specifically clicked combined rooms. So why would it give me that option if you didn't offer them?"

Third-party booking sites. The worst part about this job.

"As Selena already shared with you, sometimes third-party sites mix up locations or specific amenities at locations, and I know that is frustrating, but we can't do anything on our end."

"It shouldn't matter if it's a third-party site. You have my reservation, correct?"

"Yes. We have you booked for two queen rooms for one night. There is a note that combined rooms are requested, but as we've said, we don't have those here."

Requested, meaning she didn't 'click' anything.

"So, what am I supposed to do? Is there someone else I can talk to?"

"You're more than welcome to stay here, ma'am. We do have two rooms on the same floor, but there is no one else to talk to. You've already spoken to Selena, the working manager here, and I am the regional manager who just happened to be visiting this location today."

"Well. I'm going to let corporate know about this."

I pride myself on my professionalism, but I still have to stifle a laugh. It's astonishing how many people don't understand how these sites work. Instead of calling and booking with our hotel directly, they go through a travel website, essentially having someone else do the work for them, then get mad at us when it's not done right. Had she called to book here, they would have told her we don't have those rooms.

"That's fine, ma'am, but may I suggest you contact the company that you booked through, so that you can let them know the error on their end?"

She stares at me for an uncomfortable minute. And after a few frustrated taps of her ID on the counter, she finally gives in. "Fine. Whatever. I'm already here. I'll take the rooms on the same floor."

Thank God, I can only imagine how much angrier she would've gotten had I told her she had to contact them for a full refund, too.

Once she is finally checked in, she rolls her eyes and grumbles something under her breath in response to me telling her to enjoy her stay. The group of people that comes in shortly after her with balloons, who head straight for the elevator, leads me to believe this is a party.

"Selena, the coast is clear."

"Thank goodness." She says as she rounds the corner. "I'm so glad you were here for that one. I am too tired for her today."

She sits down in the chair and leans back to stretch. Her heavily pregnant stomach almost touches the desk.

"How much longer?" I ask as I grab my jacket.

"Any day, I hope. I'm thirty-six weeks tomorrow and have an appointment in the morning. We'll see how that goes."

"Just let me know. We're ready when you are."

She laughs. She's already told me she plans to work up until the very end, but I have an inkling that she may be regretting that statement now.

"Anyways, I'm out for the day. Let Andy know when he gets here to keep an eye on those rooms, 210 and 221. I'm pretty sure that's a party. I'll have my phone on if he needs me."

She writes the room numbers on a sticky note. "Will do, but I'm sure he'll be just fine."

I nod in agreement. I'm sure he will be too. It's one of the reasons I have him manage overnight, especially on weekends, because he doesn't play.

"Take care of yourself, Selena," I say before heading out the door.

Third-party booking sites may be the worst part, but the best part of this job? My office being at home, and the freedom to choose how often I'm on site. It's different all the time, but between six locations, it's easy to inconspicuously spread my time. Unless I have a meeting, no one is typically looking for me.

It also gives me the freedom to fit in random time to do the one thing I enjoy doing, going to the gym. I think about doing that now, but we do have some renovations coming to one of our locations soon, so I decide to head home to check on how things are progressing with those plans instead.

As I pull into the driveway, I notice Becca isn't here yet, but the landscapers are. I share a friendly wave even though I wish we didn't have them. They're not expensive, but it feels so silly. I could do this myself, but she insisted on hiring people, so it always looked perfect, and we never had to worry about it. Do I care about the yard looking pristine? No. But she does.

I've never understood my wife's need for Keeping up with the Joneses, when we don't even know any Joneses to keep up with. I didn't see a need to buy this house, as our last one was perfectly fine for the two of us, but she insisted it was time for something "nicer."

So, we acquired a higher mortgage payment (And a landscaping bill) to go from a three-bedroom one-bath ranch to a four-bedroom two-and-a-half-bath cape-cod-style house with a basement. I do like that we have a master bath in our room, even though that's not even necessary because we rarely have guests to use the other two.

Don't get me wrong, it is a nice place, but it's definitely *her* house. If it makes her happy, it makes me happy, so nine times out of ten, I just let her do things her particular way.

As soon as I'm in the door, Rex, our border collie, greets me with wiggles through his whole body, eager to get outside. We pass through the kitchen to the sliding doors, and once it's open, he takes off like lightning. He'll stay out there running laps for at least thirty minutes.

As I take my jacket off and loosen my tie, I notice a note on the counter.

Your mom has an appointment today. Be home around 6. Might stop at the store too. Dinner is in the fridge, ready for the oven if you're hungry before I get home. 350 for 50 minutes. Xoxo

Becca leaves notes like this relatively often, and it always makes me laugh because she could very well just send me a text message. But the context of this short note is the perfect example of why I do what I can to let her live the life she wants us to live.

It felt like the world stopped when my mom got her cancer diagnosis. My dad passed away from an unexpected heart attack when I was eighteen, and my only brother had just made a big move hours away, so any help my mom would need fell to us.

With my schedule being flexible, I knew I could make it work, but Becca jumped at the opportunity to help my mom out. She takes her to almost every appointment, treatment, scan, and has even stayed with her for a while on days the treatments leave her feeling sick. All while also working. And still, she makes sure I have something to eat.

She may have her own specific and sometimes (in my opinion) pretentious way of doing things, but she helps when she can.

Besides avoiding unnecessary arguments, it's the least I can do to just let her keep up with the hypothetical Joneses.

CHAPTER THREE

Becca

Struggling up the driveway, I realize my refusal to make a trip back to the car is going to be my own defeat.

My purse and work bag are thrown around one shoulder, and my other arm is encased with a row of grocery bags. Just as I begin to lose feeling in the grocery bag arm, I realize I forgot to get the keys out of my purse.

Persisting through my stubbornness, I climb the four small steps to the porch and attempt to bend my arm in an unnatural position to get the keys. Thankfully, before any real damage is done, Jimmy opens the door.

"Need some help?" he reaches for the grocery bags.

"Thank you," I say, shaking some life back into my arm.

I follow him into the kitchen, and we set everything onto the island, grocery bags now hiding my beautiful quartz countertops. The shiny pearl marble, in stark contrast with the black cabinetry, was one of the things that won me over with this house. He walks around for a quick hug and kiss.

"How was work?" he asks, his brown eyes glowing amber under the row of bright LED bulbs hanging above the island.

"It was good actually," I say as I take my sweater off.

We've made it to mid-May in Michigan. The time of year when it feels good most of the day, but when that evening chill hits, you regret letting the midday sun fool you into leaving your jacket behind.

"End of the year is here, and these guys are ready to go. But it's been a really good group. They're going to be great teachers."

"That's because they have you as a professor." He says and winks.

"Ugh, why do you insist on calling me that. It sounds so old. I like instructor much better."

He laughs. "Tomayto-tomahto."

I watch him as he starts putting the groceries away. One of the many reasons I'm lucky to have him as a husband. His unapologetic support of me, and he puts away groceries without me asking.

I don't like the word professor, especially when it's referring to me. But I do like that he loves to brag about me to people.

He loves telling people that his wife is a twenty-nine-year-old college professor, twenty-eight when I started. But I *am* only twenty-nine years old, and referring to myself as a professor just sounds too old. Every time I hear it, I picture myself soft and wrinkly with white hair and an excessively starched suit with squared shoulder pads.

Nonetheless, I know he said it because he is proud of me, and I understood because I am of him as well. We've both worked hard to get where we are now, before thirty.

I always wanted more and never wanted to feel like I was settling for anything. When we got to the point in our relationship where we started talking about our serious life goals, Jimmy agreed with everything, so it made becoming a winning team effortless. That's why we were such a great match from the start.

I knew since I was a kid that I wanted to be a teacher. I graduated from high school in 2009 and started college right away. He was a year ahead of me, but every chance I got, I took extra classes, even going to school during the summer. I ended up catching up to him, and we graduated with our bachelor's degrees together in 2012. We were only twenty-one and twenty-two, but didn't stop there. We continued with grad school and just a year and a half later, graduated together again, with our master's degrees.

After his BA, he got a job as an assistant manager for a hotel nearby, then, not long after getting his MA, he became the regional manager for the chain, managing multiple locations in the area.

Right after my BA and teaching certification, I taught ninth grade for a few years, but felt unsatisfied right from the start. Plus, it turns out that teenagers are actually really awful. I knew my age probably played a part in how some of them treated me, but regardless, I knew I wouldn't do that forever.

Last year, this opportunity popped up, and I couldn't pass it up without trying. I knew it was a stretch given my lack of experience, but the same day as the interview, they called and offered me a spot as one of the instructors in their teacher prep program. They said something about looking to bring in new, passionate, energetic people into the field to help bring in more teaching candidates. I knew then that my age actually helped. I took it with no hesitation. I was so excited for the chance that I didn't even talk about salary.

Thankfully, it was worth it, and I absolutely fell in love with the job. Some college freshmen weren't much better than the high schoolers, but all in all, teaching adults how to be good teachers was exactly what I was meant to do, rather than teaching the kids themselves.

In the midst of all this, we got married. He never technically proposed. Really, I guess we didn't have much of an engagement at all. We just started talking about it one day after we celebrated our MAs, which led to planning, which led to picking our rings out together, which led to a small wedding. And now here we are. Both established and happy in our careers, living in the beautiful home we upgraded to a few years ago. It's been almost ten years since we've been together now, and married for five of them.

I look over and see his toned body reach effortlessly into the cabinet to grab a granola bar. I have to stand on my tiptoes to reach that cabinet. Luckily for me, I don't eat granola bars.

"Anyways, *professor*," he starts mockingly as he rips open the plastic wrapper. "How'd my mom's appointment go today?"

"It was fine." I ignore the second professor comment. "Today wasn't treatment, just a quick check-in. She probably didn't even need me there. No new news as of today, but they said no news is good news at the moment."

"I'm sure she still liked having you." He slides the garbage can out of the island and throws his wrapper away.

Hidden garbage can. Another gem I love in this kitchen.

"I know you left dinner, but I had a later lunch and wasn't all that hungry, and now it's kind of late. Want to get take-out? We can eat that dinner tomorrow?"

If I had known he wouldn't eat it, I would've just saved it for tomorrow and made it fresh. Thankfully, it's just lasagna, and it should still be good.

"That's fine," I say and shuffle over to where we keep the take-out menus and mail. "Hey, did you see what came yesterday?"

He shakes his head, so I hold up the invitation.

"An invite to my ten-year reunion. 'A Homecoming for the decade,'" I read the headline out loud.

"Homecoming?" his eyebrow arches.

"Yes," I respond, reading more of the details. "It's a formal dress theme, in the high school gym this fall—like a homecoming dance."

Aren't we a little old for high school dances?"

"I don't know, babe; it might be fun. When's the last time we got to dress up and have a good time? Our wedding? I kind of like the idea. It's different."

Thinking back to high school, I always went to dances, but rarely with a date, and we never went to one together, so this could be kind of cute and fun.

"You really want to go? We didn't go to mine." He says.

"Maybe. I don't know. I think it could be fun. Something more interesting than everyone just sitting around at a bar. Yours didn't sound fun."

He shrugs. "I guess if you want to, but it really doesn't matter to me."

I tuck the invite in my purse. He may not think it sounds fun, but I'm going to drag him there if I have to. As proud of me as he is, I am of us. Shallow or not, it's my turn to brag. The boy that no one could have in high school chose me, and look where we are now.

We are going to this reunion.

CHAPTER FOUR

Autumn

I'd be lying if I said this whole thing doesn't make me so nervous that my stomach hurts.

Hiring movers was obviously my only option in a move like this, but the fact that almost everything I own is now the responsibility of strangers makes me wholly uncomfortable.

But I had no choice. I am not close enough with anyone else here to make this seven-hour drive with me, then go back by themselves. I also didn't want to put that on anyone from home. I need to get my things *and* my car back to Michigan, so what I would've paid to rent someone from home a truck big enough, then the miles here, and the miles back, it would've cost more than what I paid these young, barely twenty-somethings to do it. Plus, that cost includes them doing the labor of it all, so here we are.

I did keep the most important things with me, though, packed tight inside my Ford Taurus: all my important documents, some sentimental items, my scrubs and work necessities, and a few bags of other clothes, just in case.

Actually, I packed as many clothes as I could fit, because the worst thing would be to get there and have no clothes, forcing me to spend what money I've saved on a new wardrobe instead of finding my own place as soon as possible.

So, I pray that this trusty car I've had forever will get me and my most important things back safe. Just one more long ride is all I need it to give me. Well, actually, I need more than that, because I don't want to spend the money I've saved on a new car either.

But everything else, everything else I own is stuffed inside that giant, rather obnoxious key lime green box truck sitting at the curb.

I also just don't like being in the car for long periods of time. Road trips have never excited me. I know a lot of people who love them, but for me, they're just boring. The best part is listening to whatever music I want, but I'd really rather just get it over with. And I've always been like this, which made it real easy to avoid driving back home while I was gone.

On that note, it's time to get this all over with. The movers provide me with the general plan for their route and estimated arrival time. I provide them with every number I can: Kory's, my mom's, and my dad's. Again, just in case. With all the appropriate details shared, they are on the road.

I wipe my sweaty hands on my leggings and slide into my driver's seat to follow suit, even though I'm sure I'll beat them. This car is great on gas, and if I'm lucky, I may only need to fill up once. If I do need a second stop, it will be close to home. *Home.*

I pull out my phone. It's five in the morning. So far, we're on schedule at least. If I'm *really* lucky, I'll be there by noon-ish, well, one-ish Michigan time.

I type out a text and send it twice, once to my mom and once to Kory.

> I'm about to be on my way.

Not surprising, my mom is the one who responds this early in the morning.

> Drive safe honey. Can't wait to see you! I will. Love you.

I exit the message app and open my map to type in 1389 Kip St., Scottville, MI 49454.

I choose the route that avoids tolls because I'll enjoy more views of the lake this way. Lake Michigan: my favorite place and favorite part of being in Wisconsin. It's how I held on to the feeling of home while I was here.

The same lake that I loved all my life was here too. Any chance I got over the last ten years, I'd make a trip to visit the beach, even during the winter. There was something so soothing and comforting to know that home was just on the other side of that giant body of water.

But right now, home is seven hours and sixteen minutes away at the end of this route, which seems far, but I know I'll be there by dinner.

I just hope I make it through rush hour in Chicago without adding two additional hours.

CHAPTER FIVE

Jimmy

Weights clash as Dom drops them to the floor.

He wipes the sweat from his head and takes a sip of water as he walks forward, making room for me to do my rep.

"Izzy's going to make me go too," he says, referring to his girlfriend and the ten-year reunion.

"I just don't see the point," I grunt, lifting the dumbbell. "We already know what everyone's been up to. We scroll past it every day."

"I said the same thing. She insists it will be *so* fun."

I laugh. "Becca said that too."

"Guess we're going to have to suck it up and go have fun." He makes quotations with his fingers.

"Well, maybe they'll have fun. I'll be waiting to head home."

I drop the weights and grab my towel as we head to the locker room to clean up.

I've known Dom since high school, but we reconnected a few years ago when we ran into each other here. I didn't stay in close contact with anyone after graduation, even the ones I expected to.

Once Becca and I got serious, everything else just fell off the priority list. I had plans, she had even more, and she is a champion at keeping things in order and goal-focused. I've never met anyone who I knew would accomplish something they planned more than her. If she wanted it to happen, it would happen.

The downfall to us becoming so immediately goal-oriented was that it wasn't long before my only points of contact were her, my brother, and work staff or clients. I didn't even realize how far I had fallen off the grid until I reconnected with Dom.

"So would it make you want to go more or less if *you know who* is going to be there?" he asks. I stop and look at him.

"You know who?"

He laughs. "Yeah. You know who I'm talking about. That one you used to never shut up about."

Autumn.

I roll my eyes and open my locker. "Neither. She's been gone forever. Why would she come back for that?"

"Aha, so you *do* know who." He jokes. "Well, that is kind of how reunions work, people often travel back for them, but I heard she's not coming back just for that."

I shut the locker door and turn to face him.

"She's moving back?"

"That's what I heard. You know Izzy is always in everyone's business."

"When?"

He shrugs and laughs again. "I don't know that much, but it sounded like soon. She heard Kory say she's moving back in with her mom."

I'm sure that wasn't hard for Izzy to find out. Autumn's mom is probably so excited that she's been telling anyone that will listen.

She was devastated when she left. I visited her a few times in the first two years she was gone, but eventually that all stopped, like the friendship.

"I knew that would change your mind." He jokes again. At least I hope he's joking.

"It didn't change my mind. I'm just surprised. I didn't think she would ever come back."

Dom shrugs again, and we move on to the showers.

While the water runs down my face, my mind joins the race. I still wonder what happened to us—me and Autumn. We knew each other basically our entire childhood. Then nothing.

Until the summer after my eighth-grade year, we lived three houses apart. I remember begging my parents not to switch my schools when we moved. It was just a city over, but they needed me to ride the bus, so I'd have to switch. I was so upset. I just wanted to go to high school with my friends. With Autumn. When she convinced her parents to help get me to and from school every day, mine finally agreed to let me stay.

If she's actually coming back, I wonder if she'll want to see me. I didn't understand why she left like that and why she kept it a secret, at least from me. I still don't. I thought I was her best friend. She was mine.

I was sad for a while, and then mad because once she was gone, she didn't even talk to me anymore. Eventually, the feelings faded, and although I'd still love to know why, it's been so long, it probably doesn't even really matter anymore.

When we were kids, we'd spend entire summers running between our houses. When we were around eleven or twelve, our parents finally trusted us to venture off a bit and ride our bikes to the park. We were only supposed to go to that park, but we'd go a block further to this open field of tall grass with a little creek that ran through. Once you were in that grass, no one could see you.

I laugh thinking about how cool we thought we were, sneaking over there when our parents thought we were somewhere else. We would sit there by that little stream of water, and talk, and drink sweet tea, adrenaline high like we were really up to no good. Yet the worst thing that ever happened there was our first kiss. A quick peck that happened once. We both laughed, then just pretended like it didn't happen.

But we loved that little secret spot of ours and even promised not to ever bring another friend there.

The more I think about it, I'm really grateful to have had a childhood with a constant person like that. Once the teen years came, we were still inseparable, but it became more complicated.

Everyone assumed we were dating. All the time. 'Are you sure?' they'd ask, no matter how many times we said we weren't. I remember the first girlfriend I had was just to get people to leave me and Autumn alone. It ended like a month later when I realized that I didn't even really like her.

But actual dating *did* get hard with her as a best friend. And the same for her because of me. The older we got, the less our significant others liked the idea of an opposite sex best friend. But having grown up together, neither of us was willing to leave the other behind.

I also remember the summer after I graduated, after her junior year, her parents separated. She took it really hard, and that was the first time our parents ever let her stay the night. She stayed with us for like a week. Despite what was going on in her life, we had so much fun while she was there. She blended right into my family with ease. Everyone always loved her.

Shortly after that happened with her parents, my dad died. No one saw it coming, and as soon as I called her, she came right back over and stayed for days again, maybe another week, I don't remember. I don't know what we would've done without each other that summer. Each time she went back home to her mom, the house felt so empty.

The same emptiness I felt ten years ago when she left and seemingly never looked back.

CHAPTER SIX

Autumn

The house still looks the same, only having some brown mixed into the once bright copper bricks from time.

The lawn is freshly manicured, obviously being taken care of by someone else, not my mom. I'm sure she still takes care of her flower beds, though. She's always loved those. They are in full bloom right now, a rainbow of petunias bordered by red rose bushes gracing us with their presence for the summer.

I didn't think my excitement for being home would hit the way it does until I realized I'm literally running across my old yard. She is already standing on the porch waiting for me, which isn't a surprise considering she wanted an update every hour of the drive. Chicago rush hour was almost as bad as I expected it to be, but somehow I still managed to make it here by 1:56 p.m.

I throw my arms around her, and she squeezes me so tight my face turns as purple as my shirt.

"Oh my gosh, I've missed you so much." She gushes.

"I missed you, too, Mom." We stand in that embrace until I hear another voice.

"What am I? Chopped liver?"

"Dad!" I say as I hug him next.

I am surprised and happy to see him here. I know after all these years, they have gotten to a place where they get along like old friends, but I haven't been able to enjoy it with my own eyes. It already feels nice.

We go inside and have a quick lunch while we wait for the movers to catch up, then spend the rest of the day unpacking and putting most of my stuff in storage.

I opted to store all of my furniture except for my bed. It was my first "big" purchase after moving, and I've grown quite attached. All my other furniture was used or given to me, but I treated myself to a brand-new bed. Plus, it's bigger than the full mattress I had during my teen years.

Speaking of my room, my mom didn't rearrange it at all while I was gone. The only things missing are the cork boards of pictures that I took with me. I set my purse down and look around, realizing it's kind of eerie. Like when a child goes missing and the parent waits around for years, hoping they will return one day. I hope that's not how I made my mom feel.

The walls are still a light teal color, a color we compromised on when they let me redo my room for my sixteenth birthday. I wanted a brighter teal, a color to match the comforter set I picked, which is also still wrapped tightly around the bed. It's zebra-striped with neon teal accents, and they were definitely right not to let me paint the walls that bright.

I open the closet to find a duffel bag with pom poms in it, from the one and only year I tried cheerleading. *Man, my mom really didn't get rid of anything.*

Behind the duffel bag, I see a little black box. A laugh escapes my lungs because I realize what this is. I turn the knob to open it up, revealing dozens, if not hundreds, of intricately folded pieces of paper. Notes passed back and forth between friends before texting each other during class was a thing. I grab one off the top that says 2: Autumn. <3 Kory.

As I open the paper, slight regret sets in knowing there is no way I will remember how to fold it back up the way it was. But it reads:

Dear Autumn,

This class is the worst. I literally cannot stand Mr. Bell. He's so annoying. Like, no one cares about geometry; we learned about shapes in preschool, dude. Anyways, did you hear what Kelly did to Sam? No wonder she hates her. She should probably just crawl into a hole and never come out. But Sam got suspended for calling her a skank? That's stupid. She is. Anyways, are you coming over today? My mom's making stroganoff, the good stuff, not from the box. If you come over today, I'll come over tomorrow. K. Hyl. Lylas.

Kory

Another laugh escapes. Oh, to be a teenager again. If we were in geometry, that means this was only tenth grade, and we were fifteen. I don't have a clue what Kelly did to Sam, but chances are it was something as simple as talking to someone else too long in the hallway.

I wish these notes were two-way like texting. I'd love to see my responses. I shove it back in and pull out another, not surprisingly, from Kory again.

Hey, are you okay? You seemed weird this morning. Just checking on you. Jimmy said you were fine yesterday, but I don't believe him. Did he do something? Or did you ask him about that girl? I'll fight her if you want me to. Even if they are dating, that doesn't mean she can act like a bitch to you. Is that why you're being weird? Are they dating? I'll fight Jimmy, too, I don't care. Anyways, sit with me at lunch. Lylas

Kory

I shove the note in the box and close it, remembering what else is hidden in here. That's enough of that for now.

In the morning, I am barely conscious when I hear her squealy voice. My eyes are still adjusting when Kory comes barreling into my room, tackling me like we are still teenagers.

"You have NO idea how excited I am that this is real! I actually hate FaceTime so much." She exclaims, and we both laugh.

"Yeah, I'm pretty happy too, honestly. It feels good to be home."

"Girls!" My mom calls down the hall. "I have breakfast and coffee when you're ready."

We look at each other and laugh again. It was like déjà vu, the best kind.

"So, what are you two up to today?" Mom asks while we eat.

I watch her move around the kitchen and smile. Unlike me, she has changed. We share our hair color, but hers is now lightened by the amount of grey that's grown in. She still looks mostly the same, but I can see the aging in her face.

"Well," I start with a mouthful of bacon. "I want to start looking for an apartment. And honestly, other than that, I don't know. I just kind of want to hang out and see what happens."

Kory smiles and nods in agreement. Her dark waves of hair bounce with the movement. My mom frowns.

"Honey, you don't have to do that. Stay here. Save some money for a while." She lowers her eyes, pleading. Kory looks away to avoid sharing the guilt.

"I know, Mom, I'm just used to having my own place. I have money saved. I promise I won't go far."

She sighs. "Fine. But don't rush. You can stay here forever for all I care." We smile at each other because I know she means it.

"So, what did you miss most, besides me?" Kory asks as she drives this afternoon.

I laugh. "And besides my parents? Probably the chili-cheese fries. Did you know that the good, quiet little diners are not really that common in other places?"

She laughs and grips the steering wheel. "Good, I was hoping you were going to say food. I am starving already."

I watch all the familiar buildings pass by as she continues to drive. Nothing around here changed, with the exception of a

Pizza Hut turning into a Subway and an old donut shop turning into a Bigby. I don't know why I expected anything to be different; the lack of change around here was exactly why I left. But I don't resent it like I feared I would. It actually feels good to be here, to be home.

And the morning has been successful so far. I applied for three apartments, one that I really hope I get. It's only twenty minutes from my mom, which makes it only five minutes from the hospital.

After a few more minutes, Kory pulls into the food spot that I hoped we were already on our way to.

We choose our seats and order food right away, both already knowing what we want. I *cannot* wait for a greasy plate of bean-less hot dog chili and liquid cheese-covered potatoes. I tried to get it once in Wisconsin. The plate came with actual chili, like the soup, and shredded cheese. I never tried again.

We sit in the corner surrounded by windows to enjoy the sun. Michigan and Wisconsin have similar weather, but Wisconsin's winter is just a bit worse than ours. Regardless of the state I'm in, I hate winter. Summer is just starting, but every year the same horrible thing comes next, so I try to enjoy the sun every single second I can.

"So, what was your favorite part about Wisconsin?" She asks just as our plates are brought to the table.

"Besides the lake? I just liked being away from here for a while. Being somewhere new."

"Really? That's it?" She looks at me with disgust as she takes her first bite. I laugh.

"Yeah. It wasn't all that much different than here anyway. Just a change of scenery, and it felt nice to be on my own. Made the jump into adulthood feel real."

"Well, that sounds pointless. You could have just felt like an adult here."

"It wasn't pointless, and you know that. Plus, you already know all this, too; we talked almost every day."

She shrugs and takes another bite. "I know, it just felt like the conversation you should have with someone after they move back home after a literal decade."

I shake my head and laugh as I finally take my first bite.

While we are both fully engulfed in our unhealthy lunches, I see a couple walk in. Kory sees my facial expression and looks in that direction. She quickly looks back at me, her eyes wider than a golf ball.

It's Jimmy, hand in hand with his wife, Becca. They walk right past us, and I don't say anything to him or Kory, but rather just shove another forkful of food in my mouth. Just my luck. My first day here, and he's the first one I run into. Go figure.

"Are you going to say hi?" Kory asks. I immediately shake my head. "You can't totally avoid him, you know." She continues. "That will only make it weirder. He's going to hear that you're back, if he hasn't already."

I ignore her comment and take another bite. "So, they're really married, huh?"

She laughs. "Yeah, I mean, I guess."

"What does that mean?"

"I don't know really. I've just heard things. Like, he's really flirty. You know his personality. It probably doesn't help that you never let him have girlfriends, so he never really got to date."

"Shut up," I argue. "You know that's not true."

She laughs, "Well, either way, I don't think that flirty stuff goes over very well with wives."

"And she's the only girlfriend he's had?"

"The only one that I know of. They've been together since you left, basically."

I shrug my shoulders and drop the subject, trying to further distract myself with my lunch. But when I look up to take a sip of water, I see his reflection in the window.

We make eye contact, and he smiles. I unwillingly smile back. It's like a reflex, and I don't like it. He's alone now, and I see the path of his walk shift in our direction.

"Autumn?" he says. *There it is.*

My stomach reacts, and I don't like that either. I act surprised to see him.

"Jimmy? Oh my gosh, hi!"

I hear Kory snort, trying not to laugh. I wish I could kick her under the table.

But he is already next to us, leaning in, so I stand for a friendly hug. The platonic greeting kind. *He still smells the same.*

"What are you doing here? How have you been?" he asks. His smile is still big and bright as ever.

My hand lingers on his bicep for maybe a second too long, but I can't help but feel the firm curve of a muscle hiding underneath his Beatles T-shirt. Muscles that weren't there before.

His body may have changed, but it's nice to see that not much about his wardrobe has. Old band shirts were a staple in his closet, especially if the tag read 'Vintage.' Being 'Vintage' made them cool, apparently, even if he didn't listen to the band adorned across his chest.

"I'm good. Really good. I moved back home, so I guess I live here again." We laugh. I sound stupid.

"Really? That's great. Since when?"

"Since yesterday, actually. I couldn't wait another minute for some good chili-cheese fries."

He shouldn't be surprised; we came here all the time, and I ordered the same thing every time. Becca walks up behind Jimmy.

"Hey, Becca. Long time no see." I say awkwardly.

She looks at me in a way that also feels like déjà vu, but not the good kind. Her whole face is tight, and the smile she sports is definitely fake. To be honest, her rigid affect kind of matches the business casual attire she's wearing on a Wednesday afternoon. Her chocolate hair is shorter than it used to be, cut bluntly across her shoulder blades.

Actually, now that they're standing next to each other, they seem as opposite as possible. He appears laid back and ready to enjoy a day of fun, while she looks like she's about to take a conference room full of important people by storm.

"Hey, Autumn. Long time no see for sure."

"She just moved back yesterday," Jimmy adds.

"Oh, that's wonderful. Welcome back." She isn't rude, but doesn't seem excited to see me either.

"Thanks," I return with the softest smile I can.

"Well, we should probably get going before our food gets cold," Jimmy says as he leans in for another hug. "It was so good to see you.

"You too," I say and hug him back. I lean over to give Becca one, too. I doubt she wants it, but it feels weird giving one to her husband and not her.

"I'm sure I'll see you guys around some time," I say to her.

She smiles and nods. "I'm sure too."

They begin to walk away when Jimmy turns back around.

"See you around, kid." He says with a wink, then leaves the restaurant.

I turn back to Kory, who is staring down at her drink, with her straw in her mouth, failing to hide her stupid 'well that was awkward' grin.

Once I'm back in my seat, I take the chance to finally kick her under the table.

"Ouch! What was that for?" she complains, even though she still has the smile on her face that leads me to believe she knows exactly what that was for. "I didn't even say anything."

"You didn't have to. Your face said enough."

She laughs. "I think their faces said more."

I throw a straw wrapper at her while she continues laughing out loud, then I stare out the window until I zone out.

"Earth to Autumn," Kory says, snapping her finger. I blink my eyes back to attention and look over at her. She's still smirking at me.

"Come on, let's get you home before you cause any trouble."

CHAPTER SEVEN

The car ride home is unusually quiet.

I get lost in my thoughts because I can tell that he is lost in his. Of all the people to see him hugging when I came out of the bathroom, it had to be her.

I try telling myself it's no big deal. But his trance-like state makes it hard to believe. *Autumn Harper.*

I don't have any hard feelings towards her, per se, but I don't believe he's ever told me the full truth about their past. When we were all in high school, you never saw him without her and vice versa.

Something about the thought of the two of them and the mystery behind it always gets me comparing myself to her.

She's always been tall, almost as tall as him. Probably five-foot-eight to his six-foot-one. I hunker beneath them both at a whopping five-foot-three. I used to think mine and Jimmy's height difference was cute, but standing next to the two of them, I just felt small and out of place.

Her long, perfectly colored hair bordered between light brown and dark blonde. When she was in the sun, like she was at the restaurant, it looked perfectly golden. It sparkled compared to my washed-out nutty brown.

I didn't dislike her in high school either, although I tried. She was the kind of pretty that you wanted to hate, but she was so damn nice to everyone, you just couldn't. She looked like a 'mean girl,' but that was the furthest thing from the truth. She exuded confidence in a way that you knew she knew how beautiful she was, yet she didn't act like it. That's why everyone loved her, and I'm pretty sure that included my husband.

I stare out the window, trying to figure out why she makes me feel so crazy, but I know it's not actually her. I look over at him and wish he'd break this silence, but he continues to drive, lost in a daydream I probably don't want to know about.

Also, we rarely eat from this little hole-in-the-wall place. Why did he choose to go there today of all days? Was this 'accidental run-in' really an accident at all? My mind just can't rest.

Although I love him with all my heart, and he really is a great husband, I think of the other times I have felt like this. His work in the hotel business, while successful, has led to not one, but a few rumors. Every time I have confronted him about it, it's ended the same. 'Nothing ever actually happened.'

He admitted to 'maybe' flirting a little sometimes, but insisted it was just good customer service. He swore he never crossed the line and never would. In my gut, I believe him; he would be stupid to do something like that, but it doesn't help the feelings I get when I hear about him talking to someone else. I've gotten pretty good at pushing all of those feelings aside, but they came rushing right back when I saw her arms wrapped around him.

Once we make it home and sit down to eat, I start the conversation because I can't take the quiet wondering.

"Well, that was a sight for sore eyes." I try to mask my irritation with a joke.

"What do you mean?"

"Oh, just seeing Autumn. I didn't expect to see her back here after so long."

"Oh yeah." He says, "Me either. It was nice, though. She seems good."

"So, you guys really haven't talked all these years?" I can't help myself, but he shakes his head.

"Nope. Not really sure why, just finally grew apart, I guess."

"Yeah," I say as I scrutinize his facial expression.

Nothing suspicious, so maybe I am putting too much into this. And not that I would've had anything against their friendship, but in all these years, he never talked about her. So, if they did talk and he never told me about it, that would be weird, right?

With that thought, I change the subject. "So, anyway, I know you said you didn't really care the other day, but I want to buy reunion tickets before I forget."

"That's fine. I'll go."

"Are you sure? I'm fine going by myself if you really don't want to."

"I'll go. Izzy is making Dom go, too. So, I'll hang out with him, and you two can have fun."

Why would I want to have fun with Izzy? I don't even really like her. I only talk to her because she's his friend's girlfriend.

"Alright then. Sounds like a date," I say and smile.

My smile hides my fear that Dom isn't the actual reason he changed his mind.

CHAPTER EIGHT

Autumn

Well, so far so good.

I'm surviving being back home. I felt so much peace that first day with my parents, and even more so the second day with Kory. I wasn't sure how running into Jimmy would affect me, but surprisingly, I feel good about that too, and I'm glad we got it out of the way. The more I think about it, the more I know it was better that way rather than if we were alone.

After that lunch, Kory didn't bring him up anymore, and we went on to meet up with a few other friends. It was a really good day.

I told them about the box of notes I found, and we all agreed I should've brought them so we could all laugh and cringe at our younger selves together. That thought leads me back to the box, curious to see what else is in here. I shuffle my hand into the middle and grab one from Morgan, one of the girls we saw today.

Autumn,

Are you going to the game tonight? I hope so! There's a party after! Come with me! I'll give you a ride unless you're riding with

Jimmy. Let me know. Also, what should we wear? Talk to Kory, I'll talk to Olivia. TTYL!

Morgan

I shake my head. I remember this one. I did go to that game and that party. And I did ride with Jimmy. I always rode with Jimmy. I tuck the note back in place and pull out another one. This one is from Kory and is dated, which catches my attention. 4/23/09. Towards the end of our senior year. We didn't write notes much by then, which makes me even more curious.

Hey.

I'm sorry about Ben. Did he say why? What an idiot. He couldn't have at least waited until after prom? Don't even THINK about saying you're not going. It's SENIOR PROM. I will not let you miss this. We have our dresses and hair appointments, and I don't care what I have to do; this is happening. Just have Jimmy come with us. He doesn't like him, so it will make him jealous as hell. Actually, that's a great idea. I'm going to tell Jimmy he's going with you, and we can all hang out after. Austin will be happy. K, sounds good. Glad we figured that all out. Love you. See you in 5th hour! <3

Typical Kory. She has not changed a bit. But prom night… not my fondest memories. The note box goes back into the closet, and I search for a different one, one that I did take with me and brought back. It's in a stack with a few other boxes of stuff that don't have homes yet. I untangle the cardboard flaps and pull them out.

My collection of printed pictures from the digital camera era, a ton from high school.

I smile at the selfies we took back before you could see what they were going to look like. Mine and Kory's red flushed cheeks, squished together, clearly freezing at a late-season football game. I think that's the year we made the playoffs.

There's a bunch more ancient selfies from all different times, and some random hallway shots. There's one of me and Jimmy sitting on a bench, and it looks like lunchtime. I laugh at the difference between him then and now. We were probably fourteen and fifteen in this one? And boy, you can tell.

The one under that is me and Kory on a playground. I don't remember what we were doing, but I do remember who was on the other side of the camera.

The next picture is from the same day, Kory and I posed on either side of the slide, holding up peace signs and our lips pursed into 'duck faces.' This is definitely one of the ones that deserves the cringe laugh. Why did we think this was cute?

I look through the pile until I find what I am looking for, my prom pictures. The first one is just me. Nostalgia makes me smile as I remember how exciting it was to get ready for these dances. My hair was tightly curled and pulled half up, a common look back then. Also popular, the cupcake dress; the bigger the better. My dress was bright blue, a tight glittery corset for the bodice, then an explosion of tulle. I remember begging my mom to buy a new hoop to go underneath because the first one we bought wasn't 'big enough.'

Kory's dress was similar, except bright orange. A color no one expected, but that was Kory. The next picture is me, Kory, Morgan, and Olivia, all having to stand a foot apart because of our skirts. Then there is the one I was looking for. Jimmy and I posed like a couple because how else do you pose for prom pictures? His coming with me was last-minute minute so we didn't match like the three couples, but looking at my face in the second picture, where we're looking at each other, I didn't care about matching. The next photo is all eight of us. The three girls and their boyfriends, then me and Jimmy. We had so much fun at the dance that night. It was everything a prom should be.

I hang onto that memory as I put the pictures away, wishing the second half of the night's memories were as happy as the first.

CHAPTER NINE

Jimmy

It's been three days.

I haven't stopped thinking about her for three days. I couldn't get over the fact that Dom was right, and she was really here.

I tried everything I could to not think of her. I spent extra time at the gym. I volunteered to help with mundane tasks on-site at work that I usually don't have to deal with. I tried to find things that needed to be done around the house so I could immerse myself in a project, but with this new house, there weren't many projects to come up with. None of it worked anyways. The only thing on my mind was her.

I heard her before I saw her. Her laugh. My favorite thing about her. As soon as the sound hit my ears, all the hair on the back of my neck stood up, and I instinctively turned around. I didn't know if she was actually here yet or not, but I knew I knew that voice.

I wish we had gotten to talk more. There is so much I want to talk about, to catch up on. She still looked exactly the same as the last time I saw her, and that made it so much worse.

A whole decade. That's so much time for two people who were inseparable for so many years before that.

That word sticks in my mind. *Inseparable.* A quick Google search says the definition is 'unable to be separated or treated separately.' That was us.

People use that word all the time. Many times, for those first friends you have as kids, but usually then it's referring to a sibling or cousin, someone they really don't have an option to be separated from. That wasn't us.

We were inseparable by choice. We wanted to be around each other all the time, even at seven, and those feelings never went away.

Our parents were never even really friends. They knew each other and had seen each other often, and I definitely never felt like they disliked each other. I guess they just didn't click. Unlike us.

Once I'm situated at work for the morning, an advertisement plays on the lobby TV. Waves crash across the screen, and it does the opposite of distracting me. It brings me back to one memory in particular, her prom night.

She asked me to be her date because the boyfriend she had broke up with her two weeks before. I was aware that she may be trying to make him jealous, but it also wasn't the first time we had gone to a dance 'together,' so it wasn't abnormal for her to ask me.

Our school didn't do anything traditionally, prom included. It was scheduled earlier in the day, which meant it would be wrapped up by eight. None of us wanted to end the fun that early, so we decided to rent a lakehouse for the night. Kory and two of her other friends were dating friends of mine, so with the help of my brother, we all went in on it together.

As soon as we made it there, the girls ran right for the beach. We followed, complaining about walking in the sand in dress shoes. The soft ground shifted beneath my weight as I followed the path of glittery shoes scattered about, as they were kicked off in excitement.

I watched her laughing with her friends as they attempted to hold their dresses up, but they were failing hilariously. Her dress was so poofy, she wasn't even close to keeping it dry, but I don't think she cared.

She looked up at me, a smile spread from one silver dangling earring to the other. It was windy, and the Lake Michigan waves acted like the ocean, crashing all around her. Her curls were blowing violently, and her infectious laugh echoed above the other three girls.

I don't think I ever saw her happier than in that moment. It was also the same moment that I realized just how beautiful she was. I remember saying to myself that I was so happy she was my best friend. Looking back now, I know that's when I fell completely in love with her, but I didn't realize it then.

With that memory, I can't take it anymore. I have to see her, so I pull out my phone. I really don't use Facebook much for anything, a bunch of scrolling when I get bored enough, but I know she's out there. I type her name in, find the message bubble, and just start typing.

I just want to talk. That's it. I know nothing about how her life has been except for the fact that she is a nurse, thanks to Facebook. I type some letters, then erase. I do it again. Finally, I just settle on the most generic message I can think of.

Sent.

And now I just stare at the screen like it's going to start talking back to me or something. What if she doesn't respond? That would finally confirm it was me she was avoiding.

I think back to the restaurant again. Her voice led me in that direction, but I still thought I was crazy when I saw her reflection. Like I was seeing a ghost. She smiled when our eyes met, and as I got closer, I realized I wasn't crazy. It wasn't a ghostly hallucination in the window. *It was her. She was here.*

I smile, thinking about how great it was just to hear her voice, when my phone buzzes. She writes back already.

> It was. I agree. I'm sure there is so much to talk about. i work at 3 so maybe lunch?

I wasn't expecting today. But it's 9:00 a.m. now, and lunch would be perfect. I write back without even checking my calendar.

> Sounds great. Noon?

I send another.

> Your choice.

Three little dots pop up, indicating she is typing.

> Perfect/ Same place we saw each other last? I'm not sick of it yet. Lol

I smile.

> Perfect. See you soon kid.

Three hours feels like an eternity. Do I have time to go home and change? Do I need to? Did I shower this morning?

What am I doing? It's lunch. Do I tell Becca? There's no reason not to tell her, but at the same time, I just probably shouldn't. I know she'll stress us both out for no reason. I thought we were going to get a divorce the time I took Selena to lunch to go over performance reviews. Selena, who was pregnant with her husband's baby.

The three hours become one painfully slow blur. I spend the whole time trying to be distracted, yet still unable to concentrate on anything besides how slow time is passing. Finally, at 11:25 a.m. I decide to leave, even though I know I'll get there early.

At 11:37 a.m., I walk in to find us a seat, but as I round the corner, there she is. Sitting by the window in the same spot she was in the other day.

Her hair is pulled back in a ponytail, fully displaying her face. Small sections of hair hang down by each ear, helping her bangs frame her eyes and smile seamlessly. She throws her head back, laughing with the waitress, who is probably another old friend of hers. Everyone was a friend of hers.

I stand there and watch as the sun beams through the glass, illuminating her like she's the main feature in a stained-glass art piece. She is wearing burgundy scrubs, a look I've never seen on her before. Grown up, Autumn.

She still looks the same for the most part, but at the same time, I can finally see where she doesn't. She still sparkles like she always has, between her eyes, her hair, and her smile, but there's a sophistication in her face now. One that wasn't there before.

The waitress sees me staring, then so does Autumn, and her smile grows. As I approach, the waitress retreats. I notice she's already gotten drinks.

"I ordered some sweet teas. For old times' sake." She smiles and her lips glisten, covered in subtle, yet noticeably shimmery gloss.

"Thank you," I say, and it shouldn't take rocket science to know that I am thanking her for two things.

For the tea, and proving I wasn't the only one who couldn't wait the full three hours.

CHAPTER TEN

Autumn

You did *not* end up with a cat!" I exclaim and laugh as he takes a bite of his turkey club. "You hated cats!"

He lifts a finger. "No. *Your* cat hated *me*."

We both laugh. I remember how much she really *did* dislike him. She would hide whenever he came over, and she would hiss any time he tried to touch her. And it was only him. No one else.

He reaches over the table with his phone, showing me a picture. A black and white dog and an almost matching black and white cat.

"So, these are my kids. Rex and Rosie. And believe it or not, just like yours, Rosie is not a huge fan of me." We both laugh again.

I debated on if this was a good idea or not. This is actually so nice. I was worried about running into him, but after it happened, I realized it felt good. I was happy to see him, and I knew there was so much to catch up on, like he said.

Sure enough, we picked up right where we left off. As soon as he sat down, it was like high school all over again, and we laughed so much my cheeks and ribs felt bruised.

I watch him as he talks, and internally accept how much I actually missed him. I can tell he's been going to the gym before he says it. He isn't bulky, but the muscles I felt are now clearly defined through his tailored button-down shirt, which he didn't have before. Even his face is more toned than I remember.

Both of us are here dressed for work, and I'm pretty sure the only times I've ever seen him in a suit and tie were at school dances, which is ironic. But nothing he wore then fit him the way this shirt does. It's a good look on him.

His eyes catch mine. I always loved the way they glow in the sun. As a blue-eyed person, I firmly believe that brown eyes don't get the attention they deserve. They have a hidden ring of gold around them, and when the sun hits them just right, those rings shine, like his are right now.

He reaches back behind his head to scratch the nape of his neck, and I can't help but follow the outline of his chiseled arms all the way to his brown hair, short at the bottom and getting slightly longer as it gets to the top. Just enough to look messy, but in a good way.

As he smiles, the stubble on his jawline moves with his skin. I wonder if he is growing a beard or just hasn't shaved in a couple of days. Whichever the case, the stubble also looks good on a mature him.

His finger scrolls to the next picture, and it's of Becca with the cat, smiling and cuddling on the couch. Clearly, Rosie does have a favorite.

Speaking of Becca, we haven't talked about her at all. Do I bring her up? Does she know we're here? But then again, why wouldn't I bring her up? It shouldn't be weird. We're friends. Having lunch.

I take a sip of my tea.

"So… I was pleasantly surprised to hear you got married."

He chuckles. "You kept tabs on me while you were gone?"

I laugh it off and pretend not to feel the blush heating on my cheeks. He keeps talking.

"Yeah, Becca. She's great. But why were you surprised?"

I look at him through scrunched eyebrows. "Because you never even had like *real* girlfriends. I never expected to see you actually settle down with someone so soon after high school. Remember Sarah?" He rolls his eyes, so I know he does. It makes me laugh. "She LOVED you." Now he laughs too.

"She was crazy. We only dated for like thirty days."

"Yeah, well, she had the whole wedding planned and told everyone so." We both laugh some more.

"Well, what about that Trevor guy? He was pretty obsessed with you, too."

He's got jokes today.

"Trevor? The one I never dated because you insisted, he only wanted to get in my pants?" I joke back.

He chokes on his drink. "That was probably true."

"Probably?!" I ask with a laugh, "I should probably look him up then and see if he's still obsessed with me."

He shakes his head with a laugh. "But really, what about you?" he says, redirecting the subject. "I'm surprised you're *not* married."

I shrug my shoulders. "Just hasn't worked out. I've been on a handful of dates, even fewer second dates, and only two relationships. The first one ended right before our first anniversary when I found out he was still living with his 'ex.' Then the second one just changed his mind after a year and a half. Sent me a text, and that was that. We never spoke again."

I read the surprise in his face. "Well damn. I'm sorry."

I shake my head. "Don't be. They probably just wanted to get in my pants, too."

He chokes on his drink again. Clearly, I'm the one with the better jokes today. "Anyways, it happens. I am happy for you, though."

He looks down. "I'm sorry for not inviting you. It was just…"

I stop him. "It's fine. Seriously, I get it. I moved away, ghosted everyone, I didn't expect to be invited back for the fun stuff."

He nods, and we pivot quickly into different conversations. I try not to notice how many times the waitress has walked by since setting our bill on the table.

"So how was college?" he asks.

"It was college. Felt like it lasted forever."

He laughs as he takes a drink. "I feel that."

"Honestly, I think it felt worse than high school because I really didn't have anyone. I like being alone a lot now, but sometimes it's still nice to have someone to walk to class with, ya know?"

"Neither of the guys you dated went to school with you?"

"One did, but our classes weren't ever near each other."

"You're meaning to tell me that in ten years you really didn't make any new friends?"

I shake my head. "Not close ones."

"I find that hard to believe. Not you."

"I've changed since you last saw me."

"I can't imagine you've changed that much."

My cheeks flush. "None of the friends I made were as good as the ones I had here, I guess."

We share a smirk and fall into an awkward few minutes of silence until we're saved by the bell. It's 2:15 p.m. I had a feeling we would lose track of time, so I set an alarm to make sure I'm not late for my first week of work.

"Well, I should probably get going. Duty calls."

He nods and puts cash on the table as he stands. I didn't expect him to pay, but for some reason, I don't argue.

We walk outside together and stop near my car to say our goodbyes. He envelopes me in a hug, but it's not the hug he gave me the other day. It's my favorite kind of hug and the one he gave me the last time I saw him. The only thing that ever really made me feel better on a bad day.

My face is nestled in his shoulder, with one of his arms wrapped around my lower back, the other wrapped across my shoulder blades, and his hand resting on my head. I could stand here forever, but I know I can't. I feel him kiss the top of my head, and I get goose bumps, but don't say anything. He releases me and steps back.

"See you around, kid," he says with a smile.

I laugh, "You're really never going to give that up, are you?"

His smile turns mischievous. "Never"

I nod. "See you around then."

With that, he drops my hand and walks away, taking any and all sense I had left with him.

CHAPTER ELEVEN

Becca

Cleaning is my favorite de-stressor.

I've thought about hiring a cleaner, but it gives me too much satisfaction to know everything is done the right way. Plus, Jimmy would just have a list of reasons why that would be pointless to spend money on, so I'll save that battle for another day. Maybe after we have kids, even though I can't decide if I actually want to or not.

But for now, I love to dive deep into cleaning every crack and crevice when my mind is racing. Does it always have a reason to race as often as it does? Nope. But the smell of bleach seems to help.

In the kitchen, I sort through the mail that has gathered in the box to get rid of the pieces that don't need to be in there anymore. The invitation to my reunion is one that goes to the trash pile since I already bought the tickets.

It still bothers me that Jimmy changed his mind so quickly after seeing her. I want to believe that those two things are not related, but it's one of the things my mind is racing about at the moment.

My husband has always been attractive, long before we started dating. In high school, he was the guy that everyone knew of, even if he didn't know them. There wasn't a single girl who didn't want a piece of him, yet he was seemingly untouchable because of her.

She was everywhere he was, and no girl wanted to deal with that. The few who thought they could just have him failed.

I didn't go to parties often back then, but I remember one specifically. One that the two of them were also at.

It was after an early-season football game, like the first or second one of the year. Our team had beaten a rival that normally beat us, and everyone was elated about it. I was there because a friend of mine at the time was dating one of the players, who was hosting the party. She was just as antisocial as me, so she begged me to keep her company.

Most people were outside enjoying the warm evening, but we stayed in the house, enjoying the quiet and avoiding the impending chaos. At some point, we heard splashes and realized people were jumping in the pool. Clothes were all over the place, with no telling whose was whose.

"You want to get in?" Hayley asked me.

"Absolutely not."

She laughed, surely expecting me to say something along those lines. "Jesus. Look at those two." She said and nodded towards the end of the pool.

The two she was referring to? Jimmy and Autumn getting ready to join the other swimmers. He was watching as she undressed, and in just that brief moment, it felt like the rest of us should be in another room.

"Just friends, my ass." She mumbled and rolled her eyes. She liked him and would've buckled the second he gave her attention, but I didn't care as much. Sure, he was hot, but I was more interested in my junior year GPA than hooking up with the same guy everyone else wanted to hook up with.

"Wasn't he just with Kristy?" I asked.

She snorted. "Yeah, they dated for like two months and just broke up last week. Now look at him."

She wasn't wrong. They definitely looked more like a couple than friends. And he didn't look like someone who was getting over a break-up.

I continued watching them move together through the pool, never more than a foot apart. It wasn't jealousy that kept my eyes on them at the time, but rather just that they were both so attractive, it was hard *not* to stare. All the girls' eyes were always on him, and the guys' were on her. You just couldn't help it.

They didn't seem to realize or care, though, as they carried on as if they weren't half-naked in a pool full of other half-naked people.

Before long, they were even closer than a foot apart, him holding her piggyback style with her arms slid up under his, her hands resting on his chest. Her face was close to his, and he leaned back to say something to her. From another angle, it probably looked like they kissed. She threw her head back, laughing at whatever it was he said, and they continued like that until getting out of the pool.

"Seriously, though. How many times do you think they've hooked up?" Hailey asked, obviously still staring too.

Besides to gossip, I didn't care about the answer then. They were just classmates, probably doing the same thing that everyone else was doing.

But now, ten years later, I can't help but obsess over that same question, wishing I had gotten the answer then.

CHAPTER TWELVE

Jimmy

Six out of the fourteen fluorescent tubes are flickering.

I stare at them dancing out of synch while I lie uselessly on the weight bench.

Coming to the gym alone while your mind is overloaded is not at all productive. My phone beeps, and I'm pretty sure I have lifted this iPhone more than any provided weight since I've been here.

Autumn's response to me saying she needs to get more sleep.

I shake my head and laugh as I stick my phone back into my pocket. Maybe if I ignore her, she'll fall back asleep. But ignoring her is the hardest part. This conversation is just the tiniest glimpse into what our everyday lives have become over the last few weeks. Our conversations hardly ever have an ending, and I don't want them to.

I know I'm heading for trouble, but it's too late. I can't stop, and worse, I know I don't want to.

Everything with Autumn had always been so easy, so natural. And it still is. She fills a hole in my life that I had placed a Band-Aid over. But after that lunch, that Band-Aid's been ripped off, and we talk every day again. She can't be on her phone much at work, but her being on the afternoon shift meant we got to talk the majority of the day anyway.

We talk about everything. She randomly sends me things that she thinks are funny, and even if I don't agree, the fact that she thinks of me always makes me smile, regardless. She told me I was the first one she texted when she got the apartment she wanted, and made me swear not to tell Kory that I knew first, just like she used to do all those years ago.

After a few hours of work and trying really hard to ignore her, I decide I need to see her again. Becca just went away for the night to attend the campus's commencement ceremony, and I plan to take advantage of the alone time. Obviously, on the same wavelength, I get another message from Autumn.

Have you heard about our reunion?

I have.

Are you going?

I'm thinking about it.

Then I am too.

Good.

I am going. With Becca.

No, Becca doesn't know our friendship is rekindled, but she can't really be surprised. She's my oldest friend. I send another message.

> Can I see you again?

She reads it, but I follow it up with a third before she responds.

> Becca's gone for the weekend, so I'm on my own for dinner. Let's go get food a celebrate your new place.

> I do have tomorrow off.

She sends another.

> Okay. Let's do it. People at work keep telling me about this place over here. Let's meet there.

She sends me an address. It's closer to her place, about twenty-five minutes from here. Perfect. She sends another message.

> 7?

I look at the time. Five-thirty. I do have some work to wrap up for the weekend. My work hours have slowly crept later and later into the evening, as my mornings have become more distracting.

> 8? I have to do a few things first.

Trying to have me up past my bed time?

Maybe.

Oh. Coming from Ms. I don't want to sleep? Nice try.

She sends back the emoji that laughs with tears, then another message.

Fine. 8. See you there.

Completing and submitting a few reports, driving home, showering, and getting ready help pass the time faster than the last time I had to wait to see her.

I put on jeans and a light grey V-neck shirt. Becca told me once that a V-neck was a step up from my (in her opinion) awfully casual vintage T's, but an acceptable step down from my button-down work shirts. It felt appropriate for a celebration.

I spray the cologne I've worn since high school. Autumn helped me pick it out one time, and a bottle has stayed in my collection ever since.

I get here before her this time. The place she brought me to is advertised as a bar/restaurant, but it definitely has more of a bar atmosphere. The lighting is dim, mainly lit by neon signs and string lights.

Loud music plays, and it only takes a few jarring genre changes to know there's a customer-controlled jukebox somewhere in here. There are a few short tables, but mostly high-tops, and no booths.

I don't know where she'd like to sit, so I just find two open seats at the main bar; we're here celebrating after all.

Being here first not only allows me to choose our seats, but it also gives me the blessing of watching all the heads turn as she walks in. Everyone watching her as she walks right into my hug.

The first thing I notice tonight is her bright red lipstick. I don't think I've ever seen her wear lipstick. The bold color complements her blonde hair and contrasts with her black shirt at the same time. She's also in a V-neck, but the V in her shirt is cut much lower than mine. *Have they always looked like that?*

"Did you order drinks yet?" she asks.

"I did not," I answer and politely wave for the bartender.

I order a Long Island, and she asks for the same. Our drinks come quickly, and we tap our glasses together, 'toasting' to her new place.

She tells me about the move and how she's happy that everything she brought with her fits perfectly. Her mom cried, despite it being less than thirty minutes away. She's on the third floor, which sucked for moving, but says it's nice not having an upstairs neighbor. Plus, according to her, it makes the balcony feel fancier, despite the less-than-stellar view.

We move on from her apartment and talk about our jobs. At some point, we get back to the reminiscing, laughing in between each 'remember when?' It's amazing how many memories we have. We can talk about them for hours, and we do.

I don't know how many times our drinks have been refilled. I also don't know why I do this, but at one point during all of those remember whens, I quickly lean in and kiss her. I pull away just as fast, and she stares at me, blinking.

"Do you remember being each other's first kiss?" I ask.

She breaks her stare with a smile and takes a sip out of the drink stirrer she's using as a straw. "We were like eleven and twelve, that hardly counts."

"Sure, it does, you looked at me exactly the same as you did just now."

We both smile, holding eye contact for a few seconds. She looks away first when she asks the bartender to close her tab. I follow suit.

On the way outside, I can see in her walk that it's probably a good idea she Ubered here. Not sloppy, but not steady either. I'm honestly not far behind her myself. I guess I didn't think this one through. We walk out the door and head around the corner to wait for her ride.

I look at her leaning up against the building, one foot pressed into the bricks, looking like she came straight out of an edgy magazine cover. The rips in her jeans accentuate the skin underneath that's trying to be exposed from the pressure of her bent leg. She notices me smiling, and her lips stretch seductively as her eyelashes flutter. Her boozy smile works as a magnet, and I can't fight the pull anymore.

In an instant, my lips are on hers, and our tongues find each other. The heat from her body absorbs into mine. My hand on the back of her head feverishly tries to pull her into me more, if possible. I want it to be possible.

I pull our lips apart and bring mine to her neck. She smells so good. She tastes so good. Where has she been? She hums in response, and I think the vibration from her throat goes straight through my veins.

My mouth finds its way back to hers. She grabs my head, then wraps her leg around mine. I follow her lead and lift both legs, wrapping them around my waist and pinning her between my burning body and the cold wall.

Headlights pull in, and we quickly adjust, both out of breath. The Uber pulls up next to us, and I open the door for her, but instead of sinking into the seat, she stops and looks up at me.

"You wanna see my new apartment?"

CHAPTER THIRTEEN

Becca

The university I work for has multiple locations throughout the state, but they all come together for one big commencement ceremony.

Thankfully for me, the place they chose is about an hour away from Jimmy's brother's house. His wife is the only person I can tolerate enough to consider a friend. Three and a half hours from home is far enough to justify getting a weekend in a hotel to myself, but close enough to take advantage of the time and meet up with her for dinner.

"So what's new? We haven't gotten away from the guys in a while." Chelsey asks as soon as she sits down.

"Oh, you know. Not much, just living the dream." I roll my eyes sarcastically, and she laughs.

"Always." She takes a sip of the water that was waiting for her. "Will is really getting on my nerves lately. I needed this dinner."

"Ooh, do tell." I take a drink of mine.

"Just being annoying. He won't stop bothering me about going back to finish school. Why does it matter? He makes enough for both of us."

The waiter interrupts, ready to take our order. She goes first, twirling a piece of her copper hair in her finger. Sometimes I forget how immature Chelsey actually is, until she says something like this.

I still wonder how Will ended up with her as his wife. It's never made sense to me. He's two years older than Jimmy, but she's a year younger than me, making them four years apart. We first met her when he brought her as his date to our wedding.

She showed up in a slinky little strapless dress, far more appropriate for the club than a guest at some strangers' wedding. I wondered where he found her; my initial assumption was somewhere X-rated on the internet.

Jimmy and I were trying to enjoy our dinner when I asked, '*Why would you come to a wedding dressed like that?*'

'*Is that really what you're thinking about right now?* he said with an eye roll, then planted a kiss on my cheek. '*Let my brother have some fun.*'"

So I did, and now I'm sitting here listening to her complain about how annoying he is while she drags them into debt.

I was so sure it wasn't going to last. *I'm still not so sure, to be honest.* I thought it was just a fling with this cute, young redhead. To everyone's surprise, they were engaged by our first anniversary. It took them forever to actually get married, though, finally holding the ridiculously expensive ceremony a year and a half ago.

We started getting close shortly before the wedding, her adding me as a bridesmaid at the last minute. Then, less than a year after the wedding, they moved to their big new house in the country. *That's why he wants you to get a job, Chelsey.*

I also convinced Jimmy to move into a nice big house, but I contribute to our finances, so he can't really tell me no. Plus, our house in the suburbs doesn't come with the property taxes that theirs do.

Having to quit her job due to the move, she took that as her opportunity to also 'take a break' from school. I'm sure he never intended for her not to retain a decent income. But she's my friend, so I don't tell her that. I order my meal and continue the conversation.

"Why don't you want to finish school? Or get a part-time job at least? I'd go crazy if I were home all the time."

She shrugs her shoulders. "Because it's overrated anyways. I don't even know what I planned on doing afterwards. My major was psychology. What do you even do with a psychology degree?"

Having conversations like these makes me more thankful for my and Jimmy's relationship. We never dealt with any of this messiness.

I don't know what else to say, and the thought of Jimmy leads me to another topic, so I change the subject.

"Have you ever heard of Autumn?"

"Jimmy's old friend?" she asks.

I roll my eyes. I also always forget that she still went to our school. Younger than us, but even she remembers. Also, I hate that she refers to her as that. *Jimmy's old friend.*

"Yeah. That one. We saw her the other day."

"You say that like you're bothered by it."

Our food comes, and we each take the first bite. "I am, I think," I say with a mouthful. "I don't know why, but I just don't like her, I guess."

She looks at me like she's judging me while she chews her food. "Please tell me you're not threatened by some girl he slept with when he was in *high school. "* She emphasizes high school.

"So they *did* sleep together?" I spit out.

She puts her hands up defensively. "Oh no. I have no idea. I'm just assuming so since you're feeling some type of way about just seeing her."

Maybe she's right. I did tell myself from the start that I was being crazy. But am I really though? She reads my mind.

"I honestly think you're being a little paranoid. You guys are great together. He does anything you want. I wish Will were more like him. Even if they did sleep together, it was forever ago. Do you still care about anyone you hooked up with at that age? I sure don't." She laughs at herself, and I'm sure her list is much longer than mine.

I use my fork to slide the food around my plate. She's got a point. I don't either. And it was forever ago. So is it me? Am I my own problem?

She changes the subject and starts babbling on about which new ridiculous reality show she is into at the moment. I try to listen, but I don't really care. No other part of the conversation but 'they slept together' repeats in my head.

The rest of the dinner drags on, and I never find myself fully reengaged back into the conversation. She's probably right, but I can't let it go. I'm obviously not the only one who suspects there is more to their story, and it bugs me. Why? I guess I don't know. If they have slept together, I know she's not the only one, and I've never thought about anyone else he might have slept with. I've slept with other people, and Chelsey's right. I don't think about them ever. But I just can't shake it.

I'm still thinking about it when I make it to my room for the night. It's bothering me so much that I don't even care to text him, because I feel like anything he says will annoy me right now. But even so, I'm also irritated he hasn't talked to me all night. Clearly, it's time for me to just go to bed.

Right as I shut the light off, my phone finally lights up. I grab it, but it's still not Jimmy. Just Chelsey.

> Will wanted me to remind you about dinner on Sunday. We'll come to you since you'll just be getting home. Same place?

I don't even respond, just roll over and try to shut my brain off for some sleep.

But I can't. As soon as I start to settle, one day, about ten Decembers ago, pops into my head. Maybe this is my fault. I probably shouldn't have done what I did. But I felt the same way then that I do now, so really, I don't regret it.

I just did what was best for me and Jimmy.

CHAPTER FOURTEEN

Autumn

I lean my head against the doorway and stare at the man in my bed.

A single ray of sunlight leaks through the blinds, hitting his back like Cupid's perfectly aimed arrow. He's wrapped in the pale blue sheets, still silently asleep, and he looks so serene. I wonder if he slept as good as I did—better than I've slept in years.

I watch his shoulder blades adjust with each breath and remember how it felt to have them in my fingertips last night. *Last night.*

Ugh. How did we get here? I turn and walk to the kitchen. I know how badly I wanted to see him, but I really thought I was stronger than this.

I start a pot of coffee and sulk there with my head in my hands, thinking of the two times I let this happen in the past.

The first time we were sixteen and seventeen. He had just lost his virginity, *even though he would never admit that it had finally happened to anyone but me at the time*. I hadn't yet, but was curious, and quite frankly, too scared to do it with anyone else.

It wasn't romantic, it wasn't special, and there really was no rhyme or reason to it. It was quick and frantic in his parents' camper parked in their backyard. I could barely concentrate on what was happening, between being so uncomfortable *and* being worried we'd get caught. I was sure my parents would never let me see him again.

But it happened, and we just kept on with life like nothing was different. He never brought it up, and neither did I. I knew I wasn't willing to risk the friendship over making it weird, so like that first kiss when we were kids, we just never talked about it again.

I often wondered why that was. *Why was it so weird?* As time went on, we talked about hooking up with other people, but we couldn't talk about hooking up with each other. Some days I really wanted to just talk about it, but he never did, so neither did I.

But then it happened again, after my prom, and that time was different. It felt planned. We had our own room at the lake house. It was just us. No rush, no worry of getting caught, just the time alone.

And it felt different. We both had more experience at that point, but it felt different emotionally, too. I know it did for me, and I was positive it did for him too, as he kissed the back of my neck before we fell asleep in each other's arms. I remember lying there smiling as I felt his heartbeat against my back.

Then the next day came. We woke up in the same bed, but he got up and went on living again. He just went downstairs and started talking with the others who had stayed that night about where to get breakfast.

As a matter of fact, we barely spoke at all that morning. He left with Eric to get the food, and I went outside to sit on the deck. It was a quiet morning on the water, and I remember wishing I felt as calm as the water seemed. I sat there trying to figure out what *I* was doing wrong, a defensive mechanism most teenage girls resort to. Eventually, he popped his head out and said, '*food's here,*' then went right back in.

Just like the last time, nothing was said about what happened between us.

That night was what set my decision to leave in stone. I wanted to stop talking to him because I knew I loved him, and he obviously didn't love me back. But I also didn't want to ruin the friendship, so I just had to leave. I thought it was stupid teenage love, and with time, I'd meet someone and forget that he existed. But that's not what happened at all.

Now here I am again, trying to make sense of what I'm feeling, of what I've just done. There's no way to avoid it. Last night happened. Twice. And it wasn't the first time or prom night. It was different than both. *SO* different and with one big problem. *He's married.*

UGH.

The coffee pot beeps, so I grab two mugs out of the cupboard. As I pour the coffee, I look up to see him standing there. He put his jeans back on, but that's it. Those new muscles, now fully exposed, do not disappoint. His bare biceps flex as he rubs his hand through his hair.

"Good morning," he says with a smile.

I slide a cup towards him, he grabs it, then comes around the counter to kiss my cheek. Goose bumps slither down my neck one vertebrae at a time. We both take a quiet sip.

"I'm sorry." I break the silence. I don't really know why I say it, but I feel like I have to. He squishes his eyebrows together.

"For what?"

I stare back. "Last night?" My words come out as a whisper, like our parents are here and we might get caught. He looks down and shakes his head. It makes my gut tighten. But I realize he is smiling. *Giggling.* I'm confused and start rambling.

"This is wrong. I'm so sorry. I shouldn't have…"

He cuts me off and grabs my hands in his to stop me from pacing. I didn't even realize I started to. "Don't apologize. This is not your fault. I could've said no, maybe I should've said no, but I didn't. Everything happens for a reason." His hands move up to gently cup my face. He stares right into the depths of my soul. "I've honestly wanted this for ten years. Let's just take a minute to enjoy it and enjoy this coffee."

His voice calms me as it always has, and here I go again, pulling his lips into mine.

Was it him admitting that he's wanted this all this time? But wanted what? Wanted ME, or just wanted to sleep with me? Whichever the reason is, now is not the time to figure it out.

He responds to my kiss, and we melt back into each other, forgetting about the coffee altogether.

CHAPTER FIFTEEN

Jimmy

I really don't remember the Uber ride back to the bar to get my car.

Honestly, I barely remember the last forty-eight hours. I don't remember my drive home. I don't remember feeding the dog. I don't remember the drive back to her place. I don't remember what was on the radio, but what I *do* remember is what she felt like in my arms. I *do* remember the sound of her laugh and how happy it still made me. I *do* remember the taste of her kiss and the way her skin felt so warm and soft, so easy to touch.

But what happened in all this time? Was it like this before? It couldn't have been. How could we have gone from that to not even speaking at all? And what are we supposed to do now?

I pull into the driveway and head straight to the shower. I have a handful of times, I mean, reasons why I should hurry to clean myself up before Becca gets home, which should be any minute. *Becca.*

What am I doing? I should feel bad, so why don't I? I have a wife whether I like it or not. I didn't need to be married. We could've stayed happy the way we were, but being husband and wife was one of the things that were important to her. So I made it happen, but even that wasn't easy with her.

I do love her. I wouldn't have signed that piece of paper if I didn't, but why can't I stop questioning that decision now?

And despite what she thinks, I've never been interested in anyone else. I've always been firmly against cheating and had no sympathy for people who did. My parents had a long and happy marriage until death did they part.

I watched how Autumn's parents' divorce devastated both her and her mom. Marriage may have been just a piece of paper, but commitment was important.

So why don't I feel bad? And seriously, what do I do now?

I turn the water on as hot as it will go. Leaning my hands against the cold tile, I let the heat shock my body as it runs down my back. I close my eyes and see her. *Autumn.* I imagine her in here with me, her hands wrapping around and sliding up my chest...

It was my senior year, and we all went to a party after just winning a big game. It was unusually warm for September, and this house had a pool that no one expected to still be open. After more and more drinks were poured, clothes started coming off, and people were jumping in.

She didn't at first, but eventually looked at me mischievously and said, "I'll do it if you do it."

I didn't hesitate to take my shirt off, which made her laugh, then she followed. Once we were both undressed, I remember noticing that her bra and underwear matched. I was surprised by how bothered I was that everyone else could see it, too. I felt like they were all staring.

I wondered if she felt it too because she never left my side. That night was one of the catalysts for the hardest dating rumors we ever denied.

As the pool got more crowded, she climbed up on my back. I laughed because she didn't ask. She didn't even warn me; she just attached herself to me like a baby koala. I didn't stop her, though; I was happy she was hidden behind me. I was also happy because I loved the feeling of her wrapped around me; her legs folded around my waist, and her arms around my chest.

I still distinctly remember how good it felt to stand there together, especially when I felt her lay her head against my back.

I hear the door shut and then Becca yell for the dog, who I forgot to put outside. After a few minutes, I hear the bathroom door open.

"Hey, babe, I'm home," she says.

"Hey, honey," I respond as I finally start to use some soap.

"How was your weekend?" she asks.

"Good," I say, and finally feel a sting because I'm not lying, and I think that makes it worse. It was so good. The best weekend I've had in a long time.

"That's good. We had one hundred percent of the graduates walk this year. They said that's like unprecedented because there's always a few who can't or don't want to participate in the ceremony."

"That's great." That's all I come up with, but I need to say more. I can't be this short with her. She'll think something is wrong, and it will snowball from there. So now I lie and make up a story that couldn't be further from the truth.

"Yeah, it was a quiet one for me. Nothing exciting, which you know is always great for the weekend at my work."

"Good, I'm glad." She responds. "I hope you didn't forget we have plans with your brother and Chelsey tonight. Hurry up, please, so I can get in there myself."

"Aye Aye, Captain." I joke. She laughs.

"Love you."

"Love you too," I say as I rub my hands over my face.

As soon as I am done, we share a quick kiss, and she takes my place in the shower. I go into our room, where I can see she's started to unpack while waiting for her turn. She's also pulled some clothes of mine out of the closet that she obviously wants me to wear tonight. On the bed, I see my phone light up, and I sit down before opening the message.

You forgot something.

With Autumn's message comes a picture of my white undershirt lying on her bed. It makes me smile. I write back.

> A housewarming gift. You can keep it.

A few minutes later, she responds.

> Too bad it's not my size.

Another picture comes next. But in this one, she is wearing the shirt, sitting in front of the tall mirror on her closet door. It's big on her, fitting like a very short dress, and also a little see-through. My smile grows.

> I guess I'll have to come back to get it.

Something tells me that last message is the end of the day's conversation, but the start of something else. I don't exactly know what yet, but I can't wait to find out.

"Why are you so quiet today?" Becca whispers between bites of her chicken piccata.

I don't think I'm being quiet, but rather just trying to enjoy our dinner. This restaurant isn't the place for noise. The low lighting, classical music, replicas of famous paintings on the walls, and ferns strung along the windows don't exactly scream party. It definitely doesn't put me in the mood that the restaurant did on Friday.

I shake my head. "I'm not. Just eating."

She nods and takes another bite just as Will and Chelsey sit back down.

Maybe I am being quiet, but I can't talk about what I want to talk about. I want to tell Will about Autumn. He knows she's back, but as of the last time we talked about it, I hadn't seen her yet. I don't think I'll tell him everything, but I still feel the urge to tell him something. Tell him I saw her and she's still great.

We make eye contact from across the table, and his eyes tell me something is on his mind, too. Or maybe it's him trying to figure out what's really on mine.

We have an uncanny resemblance to each other. Most people we met as kids thought we were twins, and sometimes I think we were meant to be because, like right now, he's always known things before I told him.

At some point, I grew taller than him, so I got to enjoy being the *'bigger little brother'* for a while. I don't know why puberty hit me first, but eventually he caught up, only an inch or two shorter than me now, with a few grey hairs that I don't have yet.

"So what's new with you?" he asks, never looking away from me as he takes a drink of his pop.

"Not much." I shrug. "Just preparing to be busy for the summer, but that's nothing new."

He nods as Chelsey interrupts with something she apparently forgot to tell Becca the other day.

The girls have taken over the conversation, but Will's eyes haven't left me, seeing right through my bullshit.

CHAPTER SIXTEEN

Autumn

Blue is so much better than white.

I set the roller back in the tray and fall aggressively onto the couch that is awkwardly sitting crooked in the middle of the living room. One of the reasons I was hoping to get this apartment specifically was because I could paint.

Thankfully, my dad and Kory came over to help with the labor. Just seconds after me, she drops just as dramatically onto the couch as I did and rests her head on the back of it with a loud sigh.

"Oh, come on. You guys are young. That should be me laid out like that right now." My dad jokes.

"Thanks for your help, Dad," I say as I wipe strands of hair out of my face.

He walks over to the kitchen and refills our water glasses from the fridge. After he hands them to us, we all rehydrate silently and look at our work.

I went with a slate blue. Not dark, but not light either. I thought about grey, but then realized that wasn't the best idea with grey couches. This looks great, though. The shade of blue complements the grey furniture, and even though I still have pictures to put up and curtains to hang, it already looks a million times better.

My phone vibrates.

How's it going?

Jimmy asks.

Good. We just finished.

I reply.

Days like today are what make being home feel complete. Kory's here helping, and Jimmy's here too. Even if he's not physically.

I bet you look all sweaty. I wish I was there.

And that's exactly why he's not here.
Neither my dad nor Kory would find it weird that we were friends again, but we're not. I don't know exactly what we are, but the last time we saw each other, which was just a week or so ago, I learned I can't control myself around him anymore.

We might be able to interact in a way that would fool my dad, but not Kory. She would see right through both of us. She's known us way too long not to. Even if she didn't know him that well, she knows me better than anyone. With the way our conversations tend to go now, I don't believe he can control himself either.

But I love it. I love the feeling I get in my chest when he says stuff like that. I love the feeling in my cheeks I get after smiling at my phone all day.

I thought I could be friends with him, but the more he talks about wanting me, the more I want him.

I'm gonna Facetime you in a second. i want to see it.

No, Kory's here.

I don't know why, but his comment bothers me. He knows he's not just my friend and definitely not just like her. But then again, maybe we are *just friends*. Maybe those rumors Kory heard about are true, and this is just how he talks to all of his *'friends.'* Maybe, just like when we were younger, I've thought too much about this, and now I've hurt my own feelings.

As if on cue, Kory stands up. "I hate to dip, but I have to work tonight, so a shower is a must." She slides her shoes on and sets her glass in the sink. "Love ya. Call me tomorrow."

"Love ya too," my dad and I say in unison.

All three of us laugh as she shuts the door. My dad starts picking up our mess and leaves the room when my phone vibrates, and keeps vibrating. Jimmy's facetiming me anyway. *Screw it.*

I answer, but it doesn't connect right away, so all I see is my face and holy hell. I'm not just sweaty. I'm a whole mess. My cheeks and nose are bright pink, and my bangs are practically stuck to my forehead from the moisture. My hair, which was once a bun, is flopped over to one side, hanging on for dear life. I have a streak of paint at the top of my forehead. I wish I hadn't answered.

But then it connects, and his face replaces mine on the screen. I groan, knowing what he now has a view of from his side. And I know this because he is smiling. It's not a normal smile; it's the smile of someone who's trying not to laugh.

I would laugh too if I were him, though, purely at the glaring difference between us right now. He is sitting in his car, obviously outside of work. His pale green button-up shirt fits him just as perfectly as the one did at the restaurant. His hair is neatly styled, and the stubble on his cheeks and chin has come in more. You might even call it the start of a beard now, and I can tell he's been grooming it.

He finally lets a laugh escape, and I roll my eyes. "Yeah, yeah. Go ahead and laugh. Are you ready to see it now?" I ask.

"I already did." He says, still smiling.

"What do you mean, already did?"

"Meaning I already saw what I was calling to see."

I didn't think my cheeks could get anymore pink, but they do.

"Who's that?" my dad asks as he comes back into the living room.

My eyes widen, and Jimmy looks at me curiously. I mouth '*MY DAD*' before responding. "Remember Jimmy?" I ask.

"Oh yeah? Well, I'll be damned. Why wasn't he here doing this instead of me?" he asks as he comes around behind me to see the screen.

"Sorry, Mr. Harper. Some of us have to work." Jimmy says with a wave.

"Ha. Ha. Very funny. I do work, just not as often as you." I say back.

My dad laughs at both of us. "Do you need anything else? I'm about to head home myself."

"No, Dad, I'm good. Thanks again."

He leans down and kisses my head. "My pleasure. But next time, he's doing it. I'm getting too old." He points to Jimmy on the screen.

Jimmy nods and laughs some more.

"Love you." My dad says to me. "Good to see you, kid," he says to Jimmy.

We stare at each other with matching smirks until my dad is gone. "It's nice to hear someone else get called kid for once," I say and get up to refill my glass again.

"You didn't warn me he was there."

"My dad? He doesn't care who I'm on the phone with. Plus, I knew he'd get a kick out of seeing you."

He looks like he doesn't know what to say. Or maybe he wants to say something, but can't.

"So, anyway, about the paint?" I say and click the button to turn the camera view around. I walk around the living room to show him how it looks, then show him how the color looks slightly different depending on whether I have the overhead light on, or just the lamps, which I think is cool.

After I've shown him the living room, I move down the hallway, then into my bedroom, where the walls are still white. It feels obnoxiously bright now.

"What are you going to do in there?" he asks.

"Nothing," I say as I lie in my bed and lean on my elbow. "Not yet, at least. I can't decide what I want to do. I might just leave it. All I do is sleep in here anyway."

One of his eyebrows arches. "That's *all* you do in there?" He smirks.

My cheeks are another new shade of pink. "Well, mostly anyways."

He's still smirking, and I have to look away. I don't know why I feel like a teenager who isn't used to flirting again, but I don't know how to react to his comments. It's uncomfortable in the best way, and I mostly just lose my ability to speak.

"How can I see you again?" he asks.

"I don't know." I say quietly, wishing I could just say *'come over after work,'* but I know it's not that simple.

"Do you work tomorrow?"

"Yes."

"Damn." He says, his disappointment palpable.

"You might as well just go there and pretend you're a patient."

He laughs. "Don't you work in the maternity ward?"

His laugh makes me laugh. "You could be a lost patient?"

"What about your lunch break?"

"My lunch break?" Now my eyebrow arches.

"Yeah, didn't you say you eat in your car?"

"I do," I say, realizing he might be on to something.

"Want some company tomorrow?"

"I'd love that," I respond as the smile slides across my face.

"I have to go, but I'll see you tomorrow, then?"

"Okay. Sounds good." I say then we hang up.

I drop the phone to my side and lie flat on my back, staring at the ceiling, already waiting for tomorrow.

CHAPTER SEVENTEEN

Jimmy

The sun is shining bright today, and Rex can't get enough.

I watch him run his course in the backyard, occasionally dropping to roll around in the grass, then getting up and sprinting along his made-up track again. I wish we had less house and more yard for him, but he seems to make do.

I take a seat in the patio chair to enjoy what might be the actual weather break into summer. You never know in Michigan. Spring is the season that can't be trusted, but this feels like it might finally be it. It's the beginning of June, and the sun is fully awake. The air feels lighter, and it smells like all the fresh greenery that has returned.

Something about this specific season change just makes everything feel better. Everyone's mood is lifted as the weight of winter is finally behind us. It's a busier season for me at work, but having fresh air and sunlight well into the evening still seems to rival anything from the cold months.

Except for the dirty paw prints, Rex just stamped all over the patio.

"Come here, boy," I say as I grab a towel out of the box that Becca put here for this purpose. "Let me clean you up before we give your mom a heart attack."

I don't mind that Becca loves a clean house. I don't mind living in a clean house, and I definitely don't mind that she prefers to do it herself, usually not asking for my help. But I do mind how irritated she can get by the simplest things, like paw prints, from a dog she wanted.

She wasn't always like this, and I've never pinpointed when she changed. She has always been stubborn and determined, but not as irritable. The fact that no one can change her mind once it's set is actually one of my favorite things about her.

When we first started dating, we actually had fun. We went out and did things and talked about other adventures we wanted to take, but after graduating from college the second time, those adventures became just thoughts of the past. But there was a time, not that long ago, that her eyes used to light up about something other than shiny things.

The spring before we finished our bachelor's degrees, we went to the U.P. to see the Tahquamenon Falls over Memorial Day weekend. Neither of us was a hiker, but we'd seen a ton of gorgeous pictures, so we figured the scenery might be worth trying something new. She was actually excited about it. She went out and bought us both hiking boots, even though we were relatively confident we'd never wear them again. She got us backpacks, water bottles, and anything else that Google told her we might need.

The drive was long, about five and a half hours, but we enjoyed that too. We took turns playing music, and I made fun of her song choices while she made fun of mine. We rarely agreed on things like that, but back then, it didn't seem to matter.

By the time we got there, we were both so tired from the drive, we stayed in our cabin for the rest of the evening. But the next day, we got up bright and early, got dressed in all our new gear, and headed out to find the falls.

Throughout the walk, she didn't complain. We talked for parts of it, and in other parts we just walked in a comfortable silence, taking in what was around us. In spots that got a little treacherous, I held her hands in support.

When we finally made it to the falls, it was as breathtaking as everyone said it would be. We were more than ready to take a break, so we found a spot to sit and enjoy the view. As Becca leaned down to take her seat, she slipped and fell, both hands landing flat in the moist dirt.

But twenty-one-year-old Becca didn't get mad. She laughed.

"All that hiking and I fall *now*." She said as she smeared the dirt on her jeans and sat next to me.

She leaned her head on my shoulder, and we just sat there watching and listening to the water crash. That was the last trip we ever took.

I slide the back door open, and Rex immediately runs inside for his water bowl, thankfully leaving no paw prints behind.

On the wall in the hallway is a picture of us from that trip. The two of us were standing in front of the falls, taken by a stranger who showed up just as we were leaving. I wonder if she misses doing stuff like this, like I do. I doubt it, though, because if she wanted to travel, we would.

I grab my keys and head for my car. As I back out of the driveway, more memories from years ago keep playing through my head, but these aren't about Becca.

I have so many more of those kinds of memories with Autumn. Too many to hardly ever focus on one. Usually, when one pops up, it reminds me of another, then another. I don't feel the same sadness with my memories of Autumn. Not long ago I did, but not anymore. Not now, when she's here again, making new ones. I think about some of these for my whole twenty-minute drive, including our most recent.

I didn't expect it to happen. I'm sure no one would believe me, but I didn't go with her that night, planning for that to happen or even hoping. I'd be lying if I said the thought didn't cross my mind the minute I saw her again, but did I think I'd actually do it? No. Did I think *she'd* actually do it? Definitely not.

But there's something there. Something that wasn't before. The need to be with her wasn't like this before. Maybe that's because I could see her whenever I wanted then. Maybe it was because I was still happy when I wasn't around her back then.

I guess I shouldn't say that. I do feel happy most of the time. I definitely wouldn't say I'm miserable, but something is missing. And what makes now different is that I think I figured out what it was.

I park the car and send her a text.

> I'm here. parked by the ER.

> Ok. Be there in one sec.

My heart's thud is the only sound in this car, so I turn up the radio. I was so preoccupied with my thoughts that I didn't realize it was down until now. This will be the third time I've seen her since she's been home, but the first time I've seen her since I spent the weekend in her bed.

I don't know why I'm so nervous, or maybe I'm excited. I've been waiting for this since yesterday, so maybe both. I suppose I'm probably nervous because, well, I shouldn't be here.

She comes around the corner, and I can see her smile from here. She feels the same way about this as I do. *God, I just want to kiss her.*

But will she want me to? I don't know what today is for. Yeah, we had sex, a lot, but did that change anything for her? *It did for me.*

I push the unlock button as she reaches the door. She drops into the passenger seat and smiles at me.

"Hi." She says sweetly.

"Hi," I say back and mirror her smile.

We stare at each other for a few seconds. Clearly, neither of us knows what we're here for. My eyes leave hers and trail lower, not that I can see her chest through this scrub top, but I can see her deep breaths. It appears that my gaze does something to her because her breaths quicken.

I look back up at her face, and her lips are parted, like she is about to say something. Or maybe she's just trying to breathe. It makes a smile grow on my face as I'm amused by how affected by my presence she appears to be. And *that* affects me. *I don't know how much longer I can just sit here like this.*

She looks down, away from my smirk, hiding her own. But then her eyes look up at me, those blue jewels peering at me through her eyelashes, and it's over. It's all over for me.

I jump across the center console and grab her face with both of my hands. She does the same, and our lips are together again. Our hands are pulling at each other frantically, not sure where to land.

She's been thinking about this too, and I can tell by the way she lets my hands go where they want, and the moans that are muffled by my mouth.

I don't know if the last time we saw each other was just a fluke, or even exactly what I am doing here today.

But now there's one thing I know for sure, and that is without a doubt, everything has changed.

CHAPTER EIGHTEEN

Becca

The seven students in front of me are already packing up their things before I've officially ended class.

"Make sure you read through the syllabus. Summer courses move fast since the quarter is shorter than the others. Make sure you keep track of all due dates." I say over the sound of shuffling books and bags.

Enrollment in the summer is always low, which is nice because it makes my job easier. Plus, the ones that come in the summer remind me of myself: determined and focused enough not to take the summer off.

"Mrs. Taylor?" a young woman I've never taught before says as she approaches my desk.

This has to be her first year. She can't be any older than nineteen.

"Yes?"

"I won't be here week four. I'll be out of town."

"That's fine. You can turn in any assignments due before you leave. It's all in the syllabus."

She nods, then turns around to leave.

Mrs. Taylor. Sometimes it's still weird to hear that out loud. I didn't change my name right away; my high school students knew me as Ms. Lewis, so I just left it alone for a while. It wasn't until right before this job started that I actually became Mrs. Taylor.

Once the room is empty, I flip through the syllabus myself to see what I need for the next class. Thankfully, it's not a class that requires a lot of prep work, as it's the first class of just content, just a lot of lecturing by me, and hopefully note-taking by them.

I check my phone to see if Jimmy responded, but nothing. I guess I'm picking out dinner again. I pretty much do every day anyway, since his response will likely say *'whatever you want.'* Normally, that phrase doesn't bother me a bit, but sometimes I just want him to decide for himself.

In the store, I grab some chicken breasts, mixed greens, blue cheese, tomatoes, and bacon. We already have eggs, avocado, and dressing at home. Cobb salad it is. My phone vibrates.

> Doesn't matter to me.

Just as I expected, I hope he remembers what today is, but I doubt he does. As wonderful as he is in many other ways, remembering dates is not one of his strong suits. Right along with making decisions.

Today is my dad's birthday. I like to remember today and pay no mind to the date he died. He's another year older today, even if that's in Heaven now.

He was my everything. My mom left us when I was thirteen, moving in with her new boyfriend and never looking back. The last time I tried to talk to her was on my sixteenth birthday. I called and was surprised she answered, but then even more surprised when I heard a baby crying in the background. She was in a hurry to get off the phone since I called right in the middle of my brother's nap time. So I just let her go.

My brother. A baby I didn't know about until that conversation. A baby whose name I still don't even know. And the fact that she referred to him as *'my brother'* really hurt. She was acknowledging that I was her child, too, yet she obviously wanted nothing to do with me. I never called her again after that day.

Over the years, I've wondered what it would be like to know my little brother. I've wondered if there's more. I know it's not his or their fault, but I can't have anything to do with her, so I can't know him or them. Maybe one day, when he's older, he'll find me. If he even knows about me.

So, it was just me and my dad. We did everything together. His life revolved around me, and I knew it. He was my best friend until a snowstorm took him from me.

He knew how to drive in the snow, but the car coming from the other direction lost control, not only hitting him head-on, but also sending him into a tree. They think he was gone on impact, and after seeing his truck, I hope he was.

No matter what the official time of death was, he was gone, and I never got to say goodbye. I was well into my adult years, just months shy of finishing grad school, but felt like a kid again. I was lost and didn't know how I was supposed to live without my parent. I had no other family. He was it, then he was gone.

The only thing left in my life at that point was Jimmy. If I didn't have him, I honestly don't know what would've happened to me. But he was there, and he was wonderful.

When we got married, he wanted a big wedding. He wanted to do all the things that people normally want to do, but I didn't. I wanted to marry him, but not have a wedding. Not without my dad. I told him we could just show up at the courthouse, sign some papers, and then be on our way.

He wanted more than that and insisted I did too, but I wasn't walking down the aisle alone. I wasn't having a reception without the father-daughter dance we'd rehearsed countless times.

Eventually, we reached the compromise of a backyard wedding. There was no wedding party, no walking down the aisle, no big guest list. I did wear a white dress and veil, but we stood there in front of our immediate family, said our vows, and then we were done.

Once I snapped out of my grief, I was determined to give myself the best life I could. I didn't have any other choice. I didn't have parents to fall back on. I had to make it happen, no matter what.

With Jimmy by my side, it was easy. He supported every goal, plan, and idea. I couldn't have asked for a better partner.

But now I pull into the driveway and see that he's not home. He hasn't mentioned anything all day, either, so I am sure he doesn't remember what today is.

When will you be home?

I text him, then walk into the house. I set everything down and stare at the birthday cake I bought, waiting for a response.

A couple hours still.

He finally says.
Yeah. He definitely doesn't remember.

CHAPTER NINETEEN

Autumn

Raindrops splash into the small puddles that they've created, but as I look out the third-story hospital window, I see blue sky.

The weather in the summer can be funny around here sometimes. The sun is still out, and it looks like a nice day, but the rain persists. I love days like this, as confusing as it looks, because you know there's a rainbow out there somewhere.

I go to the bathroom and straight to the mirror. I look like I should while I'm at work, hair pulled back neat and clean, but I don't want to. I pull the elastic off the ponytail and shake my hair out. My fingers pull through it, trying to work out the crease left from being bound. I work my fingertips in the roots to replace the flatness with some volume.

When I get back to the desk, I grab my scrub jacket to throw over my head when I run to my car for my break. We have a break room, but as a supervisor, I can't actually take a break in there. Someone will find me and need something or have to tell me something they forgot from five minutes ago when they last saw me. If they can't find me, they'll probably still text me, but my phone is a lot easier to ignore than someone standing right in front of me.

My fingers tap anxiously on the desk, waiting to jet to the car. Not that I'm waiting for a specific time, but rather a text.

From Jimmy. He's coming to see me, and I can't wait. It's not the first time he's come up here, but it always feels like it is.

I don't know exactly what we're doing, but the one thing I do know for sure is that I have never been so happy. Things have never felt so right, even though I know they're wrong.

After that first visit here at work, it turned into a routine that neither of us fought. We couldn't get much time together, but twenty-five minutes a few times a week was better than nothing. We both agreed that just texting wasn't enough.

My whole world changed when he came back to my apartment with me. Even though I tried to bring up the obvious issue when we were standing in my kitchen, we didn't talk about it. We still haven't talked about it. That's another thing that hasn't changed about him.

But this time around, we didn't go back to living our lives like nothing happened. Something *had* happened, for both of us this time. Our conversations didn't just go back to a normal, friendly thing. We don't talk to each other like just friends anymore. He texts me things like *'good night, beautiful,' 'I can't wait to see you tomorrow,'* and *'I can't stop thinking about kissing you again.'*

Those types of conversations never happened before. While we hadn't and I didn't know when or even if we'd sleep together again, our conversations and our time in this parking lot made it more than obvious that we were on the same page.

Finally, a message comes through.

> Just sitting out here waiting for a kiss.

I smile. I guess that's his way of saying he's outside.

"I'm heading out for my break," I yell over my shoulder and head to the elevator.

Once I'm at the ground floor and the main doors slide open, I'm blindsided by the fact that this is not the rain I was just watching a few minutes ago. Gloomy clouds have caught up to the storm, and it is raining more, like really raining. I can hardly see, but it dawns on me that even if I could, I didn't ask him where he parked.

So, I'm standing here, my arms stretched up, holding my jacket awning, which, quite frankly, is doing nothing. Wet and frustrated with myself, I turn to go back inside to use my phone when I hear his voice. "Looking for someone?"

In a fluid motion, I turn and jump in the car because that voice only belongs to one person.

He laughs as he pulls into a parking space, and I situate myself, shaking the water off my hair like the wet dog this weather has turned me into. I should've left my hair pulled back because it's already reverted to its natural wavy state, a soon-to-be frizz ball that's hard to tame even in a ponytail.

He hasn't said anything yet, but he's stopped laughing. His body is turned towards me with his left hand still on the steering wheel. His lips are curled ever so slightly into a one-sided smirk. *And this is why we're here.*

That look on his face is why I always end up back in this situation with a stampede in my stomach. I'm soaking wet, and I'm sure my makeup is smeared all over the place. Yet you wouldn't guess by the way he's looking at me.

"You okay?" I giggle nervously.

He blinks. "More than okay. Still waiting on that kiss though."

With no other words, we both lean across the center console to reunite our lips. His hand brushes my cheek, then slides into my hair. I just know it's going to get tangled, but I don't care. His tongue parts my lips, and it tastes like chocolate. Clearly, he's been indulging in his guilty pleasure snack of Hershey kisses, and I love it when his kisses taste like Hershey's.

"How's your day today?" he whispers as we pause to breathe. His breath warms my wet lips as we stay less than two inches away from each other.

"Better now," I breathe back.

"Well, mine's not good enough yet," he says as he pulls me back in.

This time, there's more fever in his grip. He reaches over with his other hand and cups my thigh, lifting me over the center and onto his lap. My surprise comes out as both a gasp and laughter. Once I balance my straddle, our eyes meet, and I feel the seat sliding backwards. The way he looks up at me through his lashes, I can tell he's hungry, but not for more chocolate.

"I don't know what you're up to, but not here. Someone could see us."

He nods his head towards the windshield. *It's still pouring.* "No one can see or even hear anything. Even if they could, no one's hanging around out there long enough to notice."

He's right. It's only continued to rain, possibly even harder now than before. But I still can't. Not at work. I lean in and kiss him.

"Not outside my job, Jimmy, I'll be fired, then I'll have to move away again to find another job."

His head leans back with an exasperated groan. I know it will make it worse, but I kiss his neck anyway. His hands wrap around my thighs, and he cups my butt with a squeeze.

"You're no fair." He whispers.

"Fine then." I stop and push against his chest to sit straight up.

"See me tomorrow?" he asks.

"Same place, same time?" I smile.

He shakes his head. "No. I don't want to keep sitting in the car. Come to the hotel."

My head leans to the side, puzzled. "How is that going to work?"

He rubs his hands up and down my thighs. "I'll put a conference call on my calendar so no one will be looking for me. I'll text you which room to go to, then one of us will leave a few minutes before the other."

The scenario visualizes in my mind. Sounds easy enough. Still risky, but it could work, and I would actually love to get out of this car.

"Really?"

"Yes. Really. Tomorrow," he says, his voice assertive.

"I have to work at three-thirty."

"Lunch then?" he winks.

My smile responds before my words do. "Noon?"

"Let's do eleven. Just to be safe."

I laugh. Safe? None of this is safe, but I confirm our new plans by grabbing his face and pulling myself in for all of the Hershey kisses I can get in the next ten minutes.

CHAPTER TWENTY

Jimmy

Chili-cheese fries and a turkey club. The lunch of champions.

I didn't think to ask her what she wanted to eat, so I just went with what I knew. I picked it up as close to eleven as possible, hoping to avoid the fries getting soggy. I also didn't think about how it would look—me coming in with food, so I put it in a canvas bag. There could be anything in here.

It helps that Selena is on maternity leave, so we have a rotating group of managers from other locations filling in for her. It's almost never the same person at the desk.

I'm still contemplating whether this is a good idea or not, but it was definitely a great thought at the time. Now I'm nervous, but I can't tell if it's nervous to get caught or nervous to spend more than twenty-five minutes with her. Probably both.

Room 306

I send to her when I get to the room.

Be there in 5? Just walk in?

She reads it but doesn't respond. I'm nervous again. Or maybe excited. I wipe my palms on my jeans and set the food out on the table. As I sit down on the bed, it suddenly feels as lame as it looks. Take-out containers on a hotel room desk. Not even a table.

Speaking of the hotel, this is the next location that could really use some updates. The carpet is old, and there are a few stains that will probably never come out. These walls, too. Are they ever *really* cleaned? Or is this tan color just ugly? At least the bed is clean. I lie down and take a deep breath in, enjoying the clean, bleachy scent that everyone looks forward to smelling when they jump into a hotel room bed.

Four quick knocks on the door bring my attention away from the flaws of this room. I jump up and run to the door, and through the peephole I see that it's her. A sigh of relief leaves my lungs as I turn the door handle.

Autumn smiles when she sees me, but her smile appears as anxious as I feel. "Hi," she says once the door clicks shut.

"Hi," I grab her hand and pull her in for a hug. Hoping it calms us both. "I got us lunch."

"I hope so. That's what you invited me here for, isn't it?"

The scandalous look that appears on her face leads me to believe her nervousness is gone. Her laugh as she grabs the meal that she knows is hers and sits down confirms that.

"So what's your favorite part about this job?" she asks as she takes her last bite. She puts her fork in the empty container and pushes it to the side.

"Well. Now I'd have to say that this is my favorite thing about my job."

She rolls her eyes. "Besides this."

I smile and pop a fry in my mouth. I don't tell her my office being at home, because I'm hardly in it anymore. "Fine. The people. Most days. Especially ones who are passing through. When I get a chance to talk to some, it's cool hearing about different places, different reasons for traveling, things like that. A lot of the time, it's families coming to the lakeside area for a trip, but occasionally someone comes through with a cool story."

"That sounds like you." She says, nodding.

"What about you?"

"Obviously the same."

"That sounds like you, too," I say sarcastically, and we laugh.

"No, but really the babies. I absolutely love when they're all brand new and squishy and all look the same. I can't get enough of them."

"Do you want your own someday?" I surprise myself with the question. I think I may have surprised her, too, because her eyebrows crease for a quick second.

"Yeah, of course I do." She starts. "One day. My mom was worried that my taking this job and witnessing so many different labors before having my own would scare me off, but it hasn't yet."

The laugh that follows her own joke relieves me. At least I didn't make her too uncomfortable. "What about you?"

I guess I should have expected her to return the question. "Sure," I say, now a little uneasy myself. "One day."

Maybe in a normal relationship that wouldn't be an uncomfortable topic to talk about, but this isn't normal, and I think she realizes that the rest of that answer involves more than just what *I* want. She changes the subject.

"Another favorite then."

"Okay. Shoot." I tell her.

"What's your favorite thing about me?"

"Your laugh." That one was too easy, and she seems disappointed.

"Seriously? I hate my laugh."

"I'm aware." I smile, knowing she was going to say that.

"It's loud and obnoxious." She argues.

"It's loud and *infectious*." I correct her. "When you're happy, everyone around you is happy. They can't help it. At least I know I can't."

Her cheeks blush, and she stands up. "I want to show you something." She grabs an envelope out of her purse and then sits on the bed. As I join her, she pulls out a stack of pictures.

"Oh God," I say. She laughs.

"Oh God is right. Look at these."

She hands me one of hers, and I with backpacks on. We're standing outside my house, and I can't be any more than twelve or thirteen. My hair is spiked, yes, spiked, and it looks as ridiculous as it sounds. Even though facial hair is relatively new to me, seeing the lack of it in these pictures makes me happy I've decided to grow some out.

This is also the year that puberty really started and was not kind to me, as the zits on my face would prove. I almost say something about her pigtails, but it's nothing compared to what I have going on. She knows I look ridiculous, because she isn't saying anything. Just sitting there with a grin on her face.

"My first day of middle school." She says. "When we finally went to school together again."

So, she was in sixth grade, and I was in seventh. *That checks out.* She hands over another one, this one is of me and her at a bonfire. We're sitting on a hay bale across the fire, leaning into each other with matching smiles for the camera. This was a few years after the first one. Her braces are gone, and I grew into my teenage features, having shed most of that early teen awkwardness and the spikes.

"I think this was my sophomore year." She says.

I nod in agreement. I can see the shirt I'm wearing, and it is the one from my junior year spirit week. The remnants of black paint on my cheeks mean this was another post-game party, probably after the homecoming game.

There's another one under that. It's both of us swinging on swings at the park. We're swinging in opposite directions, leaning as far back as we can, our bodies making an "X" shape.

The next one looks like it's from the same day, but not on the swings. It's a candid shot where we're both standing, but she's curled over in laughter with her hand covering her mouth. Even behind her hand, you can see her big, beautiful smile. In the picture, I'm laughing too, but I'm looking right at her.

"See," I tell her. "I've always loved your laugh."

She smiles and hands me two more, and I recognize them instantly, from her prom. Both pictures are of the two of us, standing in her front yard. We are smiling in both pictures, but our gaze is only on the camera in one of them. In the other, they are locked on each other. Maybe I realized I loved her before we got to the beach.

"I remember this day," I say.

"Me too." She whispers.

"I might sound like a real jerk for this, considering how long we were friends, but this was the night I realized how lucky I really was to have you as a best friend."

It's not entirely true, but I'm not sure if either of us is prepared to hear what I really think said out loud. She doesn't say anything back but looks at me with the same look she did that night, a look that suggests that she knows without me saying it. I push the pictures to the floor and finally pull her in for a kiss.

There are more pictures to see, but we can look at them later. It's time to enjoy my new favorite part of my job.

CHAPTER TWENTY-ONE

Autumn

I sit on my balcony a lot.

It's a good place to think, just like the morning after prom, but unfortunately with a much less peaceful view. I love having a balcony, but my apartment faces the end of the parking lot, so the raccoons that occasionally visit the dumpster are the most interesting views I usually get. The fresh air is nice, though. Plus, the lack of stimulation is actually quite suitable for sitting and thinking. I definitely have a lot to think about.

The other woman. I am the other woman. Any time I've ever pictured "the other woman" in a scenario, it's always been someone nasty, and bitchy, and ugly on the inside. Someone who didn't care about anyone but themselves, but that's not me, and I ended up here anyway.

As days, then weeks, then the first month went by, it was as if not a single year stood between then and now. Jimmy's the first person I talk to in the morning and the last one I talk to before bed.

Once we started seeing each other regularly, I thought the guilt would eat me alive, but it didn't. It still hasn't, and I don't know what to do with that. Does that make me the bad, nasty person I've always pictured in my head? Or is it the universe telling me that everything happens for a reason, like he did? I feel more guilt about not feeling guilt, and again, I don't know what to do with that.

I don't know what to do. I don't want to stop, and I don't even think I can. No matter how much time I sit here staring out at the garbage, I can't convince myself to stop talking to him.

Even though I didn't feel it the way someone should, I knew that guilt was in there because I told no one. Not even Kory, I'm reminded as a text comes in letting me know she's almost here.

That gives me something besides Jimmy to think about: How nice it is to be home and have someone to just do life with. Like today, Kory needs to go shopping, so she asked me to join. I ended up making a list of my own to make use of the time, but even if I didn't, just being in the company of someone makes the errand worth the trip.

Not ever getting close to anyone in Wisconsin left me with a really quiet, solitary existence. I didn't mind it at first. I actually quite enjoyed it, until I didn't. The only ones I ever got close enough to spend routine time with were Lucas and Drew, the two jerks I dated. After I left Lucas, was when I finally started to feel loneliness again. I realized after having it for a short time, I did actually miss having someone to grocery shop with, pick out movies with, or just hang out with at home.

In hindsight, I'm sure that's how I ended up jumping into what I thought was a serious relationship with Drew just three months later, until he changed his mind via a thirteen-word text message. *'I'm sorry, but I just don't think this is working for me anymore.'* I was done with relationships after that.

Lucas made me feel like the other woman, even though he swore they were actually broken up, and she just needed a place to stay. Maybe they were, and she was the other woman, but either way, one of us was getting cheated on.

Drew made me feel like I wasn't even worth a phone call, let alone a face-to-face conversation, after a year and a half. Plus, he ended up with one of the few girls I considered a friend less than two months later.

Like I said before, meeting new people *really* never lived up to the hype.

But none of that matters now anyway, since I'm back here with Kory to do things with, and despite my refusal to be one with Lucas, I'm now unequivocally someone's other woman.

And just like that, I'm back to thinking about Jimmy. If I can trust anyone in this world, it's Kory, but I can't bring myself to tell her. I know she won't judge me too harshly, but really, I think I enjoy some of the secrecy right now. It's just me and him in on this, and I think I love that. There's no one telling me not to, no one telling me it's wrong, no one meddling between us at all. Plus, I'm pretty sure it's me avoiding the guilt I fear I'll finally feel when I say it out loud.

"So do you need to get anything?" she asks as she pulls her car into a parking space. Another thing that's been nice since being home: enjoying being a passenger princess while Kory does all the driving.

"I'm just going to grab a few little things," I tell her. "But I need toilet paper. Please do not let me forget the toilet paper."

She laughs as she shuts the car door. "Okay. TP duty got it." The lock on her car beeps as I grab a small shopping cart. "What are you doing tomorrow?" She asks, dropping her purse inside.

Tomorrow is Thursday. Thursday is one of my days with Jimmy. "I think I'm going to see my dad." I lie.

I can't use my mom because if she accidentally talks to anyone, it will be her, so Dad is the safer choice. His house is thirty minutes from Mom's, in the opposite direction from mine, so the chances of Kory bumping into him are slim.

"Damn, ok. I need you to come over and help me rearrange my furniture. I hate it."

I laugh as I inspect a box of strawberries. She was notorious for rearranging her bedroom every time the wind blew when we were teens. It's comforting to see that it hasn't changed.

"How many times have you rearranged that same furniture?"

She shrugs. "I don't know. Maybe four or five? I'm just sick of it. I need a fresh set of eyes."

I grab a bundle of bananas; perfect ones that are still a little green. "Maybe you just need new furniture then."

Her eyebrows grow tall with excitement. "That's a great idea! Let's go shopping then."

I shake my head as we move towards the avocados. "Maybe Friday before work."

The first avocado I grab is too hard, so I put it back and grab another. Once again, not ripe enough. As I look up to try a different spot in this mound, my eyes meet Jimmy's two stands over, holding a bag of apples.

He smiles, and I know I smile back before looking away. My stomach twitches, and I try to focus back on the problematic fruit in front of me. Except that doesn't happen because I feel him still staring, so I look up again, and I was right, still staring shamelessly.

But in those quick seconds, I know we've messed up. I look away from him to Kory, still right next to me, now looking back and forth between me and him.

"The avocados suck today. I'm good." I quickly turn the cart around to walk in the other direction. My phone buzzes in my back pocket, and I know it's from him before I pull it out to read it.

> Who knew someone could make fondling avocados look sexy?

"Autumn Meredith Harper, what is going on right now?" Kory demands.

I slide my phone back in my pocket and take a step, but she stops. Her eyes and folded arms are full of accusation.

"What do you mean?"

"I mean, I know you and I know him. I know both of you, and if you tell me nothing is going on, I know you're lying."

I push the cart forward, trying to walk again, but she grabs it.

"Oh no. You're not getting out of this one. I saw him taking your clothes off with his eyes, and you smiled like an idiot at your phone immediately after. It was him, wasn't it?"

Honestly, I'm surprised I managed the secret for this long, she's right. We're busted. I cave and nod my head.

"Oh my GOD, Autumn!" she says louder than I'd like her to. I keep walking to get farther away from him.

"Have you guys like actually..." she pauses, tightening her lips together and nodding her head towards me. I just respond with another nod.

"Oh…my…God." She says slower this time.

"Will you stop saying that?"

"I'm sorry. I'm just surprised, yet I'm not, yet I still am. Autumn! He's…"

I cut her off. "I know, K."

"Wow. I just… You really moved back with a bang, literally." She laughs at her joke. "Let me see it."

"See it? See what?"

She holds her hand out. "Your phone. Gimmie."

"Why?"

"Because clearly, you've been hiding something big from me, and I want to know everything. Now. I need to catch up."

I roll my eyes, but hand her my phone in defeat. This will probably be easier than answering all her questions.

"Wait." She says as she grabs it from me. "You guys didn't like send anything nasty, did you? I'd rather not see that."

"No. You're good. Nothing you can't handle."

She nods and begins her investigation. As we walk, I look over at her a few times, watching her eyes both shrink and grow as she reads through every conversation.

"Well," she starts as she hands me the phone back. "You know this is messed up, right?"

I nod my head. I've somehow managed to still not say any of this out loud. I just keep my communications to one, now shameful motion of my head.

"And there's a good chance this will end badly, like *really* badly."

I nod again. She doesn't say anything else for a few minutes. Clearly, she just needed a short time to process the fact that her best friend is having an affair with a married man, because her next question is

"So, is it better than back then?"

"Oh my God, Kory."

She laughs. "What? I'm just asking. Is it like, worth it at least?"

"Definitely worth it," I whisper.

We both laugh together as we go back to walking and let the subject naturally change. I know it will come up again at some point, but this introduction is good enough for now.

Once we think we have everything we came for, we start walking towards the front. As we pass one of the aisles, a cart comes out, almost colliding with ours. Jimmy is pushing it. I pull ours back, motioning for him to go, trying my best not to smile anything other than a *'friendly stranger passing another stranger in the store'* smile this time.

But he doesn't do the same, and as his smile stretches across his lips, it just gets sexier. He motions for us to go instead, and I nod in response and push forward, awkwardly avoiding any conversation.

"Excuse me, sir." Kory calls out behind us. "Please stop staring at my friend, she's taken."

I pull on her arm. "Girl, shut up, come on." She laughs, amused with herself.

We get in line, and I pay for my stuff first. Once we're in the car and start loading everything in, I notice I have a text.

> Taken huh?

I text him back.

> Yeah, she's talking about you dork. She figured it out.

> Oh.

His short response leads me to believe that he's not thrilled with the fact that someone knows. I guess I can't blame him, but it's a little sting in my gut I didn't expect.

> Don't worry. It's just Kory.

I send another.

> Wait a minute. Were you jealous?

Maybe.

"What are you doing out there?" Kory calls out the window. I shove the cart away and jump into the passenger seat. "He didn't like my taken comment?" she asks, clearly already aware of what is distracting me.

"Just drive, Kory." I shake my head with a laugh.

It's not until I am home and have all the stuff put away that I realize I forgot the toilet paper.

CHAPTER TWENTY-TWO

Becca

-Pick up dry cleaning
-Get new mop heads and bleach
-Pick up prescription
-Schedule Jimmy regular barber appointments

If he insists on keeping that hair on his face, he can at least keep it neat and presentable. I already have to remind him about getting haircuts.

I compare my day's to-do list to my planner and thankfully, this is all I have going on today. I slide the planner into my work bag and grab my purse. On Thursdays, I only have two morning classes, so my day is over by twelve-thirty. I could stay back and grade papers or prepare for my next class, but I prefer to do that at home most of the time. Who wouldn't?

I guess Jimmy. It used to be nice to finish my early days at home because he was at home a lot too. Once upon a time, we used to sit in the office together and work while talking and keeping each other company, but lately it seems like he'd rather be at work.

I shut the classroom lights off and head to my first stop, the dry cleaners. I only use the dry cleaners for his work clothes and a few of my work shirts, which Jimmy thinks is another pointless expense. I do it anyway because if I don't care what he looks like, who will? He certainly doesn't seem to.

Maybe I'm too hard on him about that kind of stuff, but he's crazy to think that appearances don't matter. Who's going to take a senior manager seriously if they don't look any different than the Joe Schmo behind the desk? I wouldn't.

After I pick up the clothes, I go to the pharmacy for his mom's prescription. Things are going good for her right now, so I don't see the need to keep doing everything for her, but she's used to it, so she still asks.

Fifteen minutes later, I pull up to her house, a small brick ranch, like the rest in this neighborhood. Her yard is the nicest one in sight, though, thanks to her daughter-in-law, who paid the landscapers to take care of hers too, knowing she couldn't do it herself even at her healthiest.

"Linda," I call out as I let myself in. I find it rude not to knock, but she's always insisted I just come in, so eventually I gave in.

"I'm in here," she responds, presumably from her bedroom, where she usually is.

I walk down the short hallway and, as expected, she's in her La-Z-Boy with HGTV on the TV, a crossword book in her hand, and her cat Pickles on her lap. A horrendous name, but she said she couldn't bring herself to change the name the wonderful people at the shelter gave her. "Oh, thank you, sweetie." She says as I set the orange bottle on her nightstand.

"How are you today?" I ask her.

"Oh, I'm fine." She says, although that's what she always says, even when she's not.

"Good. Are you sleeping okay?"

"As good as I can, I guess." She smiles, and her eyes seem to glisten. I may believe her today.

Jimmy got his eyes from her; they're identical. Both he and his brother look a lot like her. Her hair was once brown like theirs, although it's now grey and thinned, usually hidden under a hat.

"Can I ask you something?" she asks as I start making my way towards the door. My body tenses because my hope was to be in and out of here as soon as possible.

"Sure," I say anyway and turn back to face her.

"How's Jimmy? I feel like I haven't seen or heard from him in ages." *Me either.*

But I'm relieved at her question, because that's an easy one to get out of, even if I'm not sure that I believe my own answer.

"He's fine. Just been working a lot lately."

"You two." She rolls her eyes. "That's all you guys do is work."

"You know how we are," I say, uninterested in hearing her go on and on about how we should slow down sometimes and enjoy life. A rant she's gone on many times before.

She's not wrong, but despite what she thinks, we used to spend a lot of time together. Even if we were working, we could work together, and it was nice. Sometimes we'd both even work into the evening, clicking on our laptops parallel to each other while chatting over dinner. It may not be for everyone, but for us, it worked.

Lately, though, he's rarely home when I am, working later on site than he ever has before. When he is there, the chatting is slim to none. I've tried to give him the benefit of the doubt, but I've just about run out of that.

"I hope you two can still find time to enjoy… each other," Linda says, reminding me I'm still here. *Oh, no. We're definitely not going there.*

"Everything is fine, Linda. I promise." I'm not sure that I *should* promise her that, but it makes her smile again. "I have a couple of things I need to do today, so I have to head out, but I'll see you Monday?" I say as I turn back for the door.

"Are you sure? I thought it was Wednesday?"

I stop and roll my eyes while she can't see them. It frustrates me that she always questions me about her appointments. I wonder if she is actually that confused, or if she just likes to test me to make sure I know what I'm doing. *I always know what I'm doing.*

"Yes, I'm sure it's Monday."

"Hmm. Maybe I'm confused. You're probably right." *Of course I am.*

"When I get to the car, I'll check my planner to see if it will make you feel better. I'll send you a picture of it."

"That would be great. Thank you, Becca."

"You're welcome," I say and head for the car.

I know without a doubt that it's Monday, but if I don't confirm with her, she'll call me in half an hour. I drop into the seat and grab my bag from the back. I flip the July tab with my finger to open the month. There it is, just as expected: Linda appt. 2:15, in the little rectangle for Monday, July 20th. I open the camera app on my phone to take a picture for her when something else catches my eye.

A little red dot on the Thursday that just passed. Four days ago. There's only one thing I track with a little red dot in my planner, something that's always been on time. Until now, I guess.

My period.

CHAPTER TWENTY-THREE

Jimmy

I hear Becca come in the door, but neither Rex nor I move from our spot.

He looks up at me, knowing the minute she sees him on the couch, she'll shoo him away. I pat him on the head, reassuring him that I'm cool with his company, and he lays back down on my leg. There's rustling in the kitchen, and I wait for her to say hello, but she doesn't right away. When she does make it into the living room, she does exactly what we expected her to.

"Rex! No. Get down. Jimmy, why do you let him up there?"

"Well, hello to you, too."

"I don't want our furniture to smell like dog Jimmy." She brushes off the couch and fluffs the throw pillows aggressively before putting them back in their assigned seat.

"Honey, he lives here. If he were going to make it smell like anything, he would have already."

"Shampooing a rug is much different than thoroughly cleaning the suede material of a couch." She looks at me like I should already know that.

"Whatever you say," I tell her, knowing I'm going to let him do it again the very next time she's gone.

She wanders back into the kitchen, and my phone buzzes.

One day. That's all I want.

A text from Autumn talking about a house with a wraparound porch to sit on. One with a big yard to enjoy and near the lake, so she can go whenever she wants. She said a house on the lake would be too expensive, but five to ten minutes away? Perfect. *And I love that about her.*

Me too. Rex would love a bigger yard. And he loves going to the beach too.

He does love the beach, but I've only been able to take him there three times in his three years of life. I'm sure you can guess why. He was a mess of sand and wet dog fur when we got home, and that was an argument I stopped having.

I bet he does. I wish I could go.

We will one day.

God, I hope that's true.
"Are you staying home for dinner tonight?" Becca calls out.
"Why wouldn't I?" I respond.
"You've barely been home lately, so I didn't know."
I roll my eyes. "I'm home every day."
I get up from the couch and go into the kitchen. She's moving around quickly, almost frantically, and her cheeks are pink. She doesn't acknowledge my presence in the room, just continues to pace around me, looking disheveled. She's pulling out ingredients for spaghetti, which is the meal she makes when she's had a long day or doesn't feel like cooking. *It takes no thought and twenty minutes to get done*, she's said before.
"You okay?" I ask.
"I'm fine," she snaps.

I take her response as a cue to back off and head for the bedroom. She's clearly not fine, but she doesn't want me to know. She may not even know, so I don't say anything else.

I text Autumn again.

> I miss you.

> I miss you too.

She sends back right away. So just as quick, I respond.

> I miss your voice. I wish it was tomorrow.

My phone vibrates again, five seconds later.

> So you don't miss my voice too?

I text back, poking at her. Messing with her is fun because she messes right back. She doesn't get angry.

> I miss more than your voice ;)

Winky face.

"Hey," Becca's voice makes me jump. She squints her eyes at me, given my reaction. "What was that about?"

"Nothing. You just caught me off guard. I was reading an email from the architect."

"Oh," she says, standing against the door frame, arms folded in front of her, staring at me, then at my phone. "Well, since you're on your phone so often anyway, you should call your mom sometime. She misses you."

"That's a good idea," I say, ignoring whatever she is insinuating.

She gives me one last look before walking away. "Dinner's almost done," she calls out as she walks down the hallway.

Any response I have to Autumn's text will lead me somewhere I'm not prepared to go with Becca popping in on me. So, I exit out of our messages and call my mom.

"Well, I'll be," she says when she answers.

"Hi, Mom." I laugh.

"She came right home and told you to call me, huh?"

"Of course not." I fib. "I just missed you."

"Yeah, Yeah. I miss you too. How are you? Becca said you're working a lot again."

"Yeah, I am. But I'm good, though. How are you doing? I heard things are looking positive. Are you *feeling* positive?"

She laughs. "Yes, everything is fine, but I don't want to talk about me. I want to hear about you."

My mom. Stubborn as ever. She never wants to be the center of attention, no matter what significant life event she's going through. Her quick persistence this time seems strange, though, like she's looking for specific information without asking the actual question.

"There's not much to hear, ma. She's right. I've been working a lot, covering a few different things at the moment."

She sighs. "I wish you wouldn't do that. You need some fun in your life, don't you think? All you guys have ever done is worked."

"I do have fun. It's just not the same type of fun you're thinking of."

"Yours and Becca's type of fun is not the same type of fun as anyone thinks, hun." She pauses. "Anyways, guess who I ran into the other day?"

"Who's that?" I ask as I move towards the dresser to finally change out of my work clothes.

"Andrea" *Autumn's mom.*

"That so?" I respond, unsure of where she's going with this.

"And you know what she told me?"

I laugh at her needing to ask these additional questions to get to the point, per usual. "What's that, ma?"

"Autumn's moved back home."

I smile. "I know."

"You know?" I can hear in her response that she's smiling too.

"Yes, we ran into her a little while ago. I think it was her first day back, actually."

"You and Becca did?"

"Yeah, we were at the diner over on Main Street. She was eating lunch with her friend, and we were picking up food."

"How is she?" she asks with a new pep in her voice. "Andrea said she's done well for herself, too."

"She is good. We didn't talk long, but it was nice to see her."

If only I could tell her the whole truth. Judging by the tone in her voice now, she might not even be shocked, but this is all she needs to know at the moment.

"Oh, that's lovely. I'm so happy you guys reunited. Will you see her again? Please tell her I said hi."

I laugh and continue to lie. "I don't know, but if I do, I will tell her."

"Good. She was just the sweetest girl, wasn't she?"

"Yeah, ma, she was."

I think I've figured out her actual reason for wanting to chat, but I feel like it's time to get out of this conversation at least while I'm home with Becca.

"I think dinner might be done soon, so I'm going to get ready to eat. I'll call you in a few days?"

"I'd love that." She says. "But I'd also love to hear more from you next time than just working so damn much."

I laugh. "Okay. Mom. Love you."

"Love you too, dear."

There is so much besides work that I could tell her. Stuff I'd actually like to tell her all about, and maybe, one day, I will.

But right now, whatever I want to tell her, and more importantly, whatever my mom is up to, will have to wait because my wife is summoning me for dinner.

CHAPTER TWENTY-FOUR

Autumn

By the time Friday gets here, Kory's changed her mind about furniture shopping.

Switching the accent chairs from her bedroom and the living room was apparently enough of a change for now. The change in plans works out for my mom, who has been trying to get me over for a couple of weeks. I normally don't like to go over before work, because it takes me further from the hospital, but I figured it's about time.

"Mom, you didn't have to do this," I say in response to the full breakfast spread already on the counter.

"Oh, shush." She says with a hug. "I couldn't decide what to make, so I made it all. Let's brunch."

I can't help but smile sitting here with her. We haven't said much since we sat down, but the grin on her face hasn't left, despite rotating forkfuls of food. Hanging out with my mom feels different now. I don't know if it's just because of all the time we've missed, or because I'm an adult, but it feels nice. It feels like I'm with a friend. I remember having dinner like this as a kid on the weekends. We sat at the same table, in the same spots, just me and her. Even before she and my dad separated, he worked a lot of the weekends, so it was us two.

"What are you thinking about?" she asks, reading my mind.

"The times we used to do this when I was a kid. I don't think you ever made this much food, though."

She laughs. "I think you're right. You might have to come back tomorrow and help me finish it."

"I might be able to do that."

"At least take some with you to work. Everyone loves breakfast for dinner."

"Sounds good. Thanks, Mom."

Her smile mirrors mine, and I know we're both equally filled with gratitude for this moment. "So, how's everything going?"

"With what?" I ask, slightly fearful.

She shrugs. "I don't know, with everything. Work, your new place, any new people I need to know about?"

I laugh, relief escaping. I don't know how she would know, but for a second, I think she does. "Good, actually. I love my job. Most of the people are great. I love the apartment too, but no, no new people."

"Not even neighbors? None of them cute?"

"No, Mom. Not even neighbors. I really haven't seen anyone around there. It's a really quiet place. That's what I love about it."

She gets up and starts clearing the table. "I guess if that's what you like. It's *too* quiet around here."

"What can I say?" I join her in cleaning the kitchen. "You know I like my solitude."

"You might change your mind if you meet someone."

"Maybe."

"There's this boy at the market here, he's real cute."

"Mom." I protest.

She gets my point and smiles, then turns the water on. I take this as my opportunity to end the conversation because she's kind of right.

I want so badly to tell her about Jimmy. I want to tell her how I would actually like to spend every minute with someone. I want to tell her how good things really are right now. But it's a crap situation. I know my mom would be happy for me, but I don't think a person with a wife is the cute boy she's imagining for her daughter.

And now that I'm thinking about him, I miss him. I look at my calendar to see the next day I'll see him. The hotel days are my favorite.

When we meet, one of us grabs lunch on the way there. We eat together, then get lost in each other in the privacy of a room. Inside those rooms, it feels so real. We don't have to look over our shoulders. We don't have to be quiet. We don't have to pretend we are just friends. We can just be us and be together.

I love those days, and I never want them to end. One in particular is my favorite so far: the day he almost told me he loved me. He didn't, but I know he came close.

I was lying on the bed in a T-shirt and underwear, eating blueberries out of the package. He walked out of the bathroom with just a towel wrapped around his waist.

I expected him to climb into the bed, but he didn't. He just stood there staring at me, so I smiled and threw a blueberry at him. Incredibly, he caught it in his mouth. We both laughed, then he finally crawled onto the bed, hovering over me.

"Can I help you?" I asked while giggling.

"Nope. I just still can't believe this is real. I missed you so much, you have no idea."

"I think I do," I responded and leaned up to kiss him, but he pulled back.

"Nope, not yet. I still have about six or so years of looking at you to catch up on."

We both laughed, but then he got serious again. He ran his thumb along my jaw, then across my lips. We stared at each other for a few minutes before either of us said anything else. His eyes were hypnotizing, and I couldn't look away.

That's when I knew. I saw all I needed to see in the look in his eyes. Nothing else needed to be said.

"You know I've told you so many of the things that I love about you, but I don't think I've ever included your face on that list."

I laughed again. Why did he keep making me laugh in moments like this?

"I'm serious." He protested. "You're beautiful. And after all this time, I don't think I've ever said that to you."

And I was pretty sure he was right. I didn't think he ever had either. There were plenty of times that he told me my outfit looked fine, or if we were dressed up, he'd say I looked good, but never has he said out loud that *I'm* beautiful.

"I don't think so either," I whisper. "Say it again."

He smiled and kissed my shoulder. "You're beautiful…" he kissed my collar bone, "And amazing…" he kissed my cheek, "And gorgeous…" he kissed my lips, "And perfect."

I thought he was going to kiss me again, but he didn't. He was staring again. I reached up and put my hand on his cheek, and he leaned into my palm, closing his eyes. "Autumn Harper, you're the best person I've ever known." He said.

I couldn't take any more without crying, so I pulled him into a kiss, but that time I didn't let him stop…

Inevitably, those lovely couple of hours had to end. I head to work, and he goes on with his life. Both of us counting down to the next chance we have with each other.

We rarely talk about Becca. Sometimes it feels like she isn't real. I like to pretend that she isn't. But then, occasionally, a reality check hits when there is an emergency phone call, or a story comes up during our lengthy conversations that reminds us both that she is very much real.

I can also tell when they have had an argument or are just not having a good day. His mood will be off, and he's very easy to read. We are always able to fix it, but I can still tell. It does make me wonder sometimes, and I think about asking him what's going on with them, but I don't. Nothing else in the world matters when we are together. Nothing else matters when he looks at me. Nothing else matters at all anymore. Nothing except for him.

Something about him completes me, and at some point, that was enough to shatter my moral compass.

CHAPTER TWENTY-FIVE

Becca

At what age does a midlife crisis begin?

Or is it normal for people to just wake up one day and not be themselves anymore?

Thank God I volunteered to teach summer classes, because I can barely stand to be around Jimmy lately. In a few short months, I've turned into Chelsey, finding myself annoyed all the time, at just about everything he does. He barely talks anymore, and I haven't cared to either, so truthfully, I don't know if it's him having the crisis or me.

Either way, I further appreciate working for a university and having the option to work in the summer because I may feel like Chelsey, but I could never in my life sit around all day like her. Plus, I still can't let go of my conversation with her that night, so I know at least part of the problem is me. I blame it on pregnancy hormones. It explained my sudden change of attitude and distaste for everyone around me, including my husband.

It made sense. From what I've heard about pregnancy, it would explain a lot of what I felt. My obsession with what he was or wasn't doing. My notice of his sudden lack of interest in doing things for me that he would normally do, without me asking first, at least. Always feeling irritable and not being able to sleep.

My period not showing up finally gave me the excuse I had been looking for. But then the test was negative, so that excuse went out the window. I wasn't even sure if I was sad or happy that it was negative.

My period stayed away for a second week, so I took another test, but that one was negative too. I still wasn't sad, just disappointed I didn't have another excuse for how I felt. I also thought that if I were pregnant, he would start doting on me again, but almost three weeks late, my period finally came, confirming it was just me and my messed-up attitude.

But it can't be just me, because he hasn't even noticed, at least he hasn't said anything. He hasn't seemed to notice a difference, even though I know there is one. His attitude lately just mirrors mine, and it drives me nuts. *There is something wrong with your wife, idiot. Do something!*

But there's nothing.

It's times like these that I kind of wish I had more friends to talk to. Chelsey isn't the best to have serious conversations with. She's too air-headed to really consider anyone else's perspective but her own.

The only other person I really see is his mom. I'm surely not going to talk to her about her son being an asshole while she sits there getting chemotherapy. And I'm especially not going to sit there and talk to her about my hidden concerns about the girl, I'm sure she *'just loved'* like everyone else. I never felt like she liked me much, which is why I volunteered to help her when she got sick. So this is definitely not a topic I'll be talking to her about any time soon.

So, I don't talk to anyone but Rosie and Rex, and I'm pretty sure even they are getting sick of me.

I'm sitting in the office he hardly uses anymore, grading papers, when I hear him get home. It's only 3 p.m. Check-in time. When he's at a site, he's normally not home this early. I hear him stop in the doorway.

"Hey," he says.

"Hey," I copy.

"How's it going?"

I roll my eyes as far in my head as they will go. *Why does that come off as such a weird thing to ask your wife? Maybe because you barely speak to her?*

"Just grading papers, you?"

"Good. I'm going to get in the shower."

I finally turn around to look at him and notice his hair isn't styled as it usually is for work, and he's not wearing a tie. As a matter of fact, the top two buttons are unbuttoned.

"Long day at work?" I ask.

"Yeah." Is all he says.

"Want to tell me about it?"

"Not really much to tell. Just a long day." He says before walking away.

"Good to see you too. Missed you. Love you." I mumble sarcastically to myself as I hear the water turn on.

I drop the pen down on the desk and lean my head back on the chair, covering my face with my hands. *Relax Becca.*

I try to tell myself. *It's not what you think.*

I squeeze my eyes tightly shut. *But what if it is?*

The elephant in the room has taken over our whole house. Nothing has been the same since he saw her, and that's exactly why I did what I did.

It was mid-December 2009. My birthday weekend. Jimmy and I had been together for about four months and took advantage of the break from school to get away for the night. His brother got us a hotel room. It wasn't anything fancy, but it wasn't one of our parents' houses either.

Jimmy was in the shower, like he is now, when his phone rang. I'd never looked at his phone before. I'd never felt the need to, but something this day told me I should. I waited until it stopped ringing to be nosey. By the time I reached the other side of the bed, it lit up again. That time, a text. From Autumn.

> Hey. I'm sorry I know it's been a while and you're probably mad at me, but I just want to talk. I miss you. Call me back please.

I blinked as I stared at the phone. She was the missed call, too. That was the first time I realized how she really made me feel. *Why was she reaching out to him? Did she know about me?* It was Christmas break, so she was probably back home and wanted to see him. *No. That wasn't happening. He had finally just stopped talking about her.*

My fingers were shaking as I deleted the message, the missed call, then blocked her number. After carefully setting the phone back down exactly how it was, I rushed back over to where I was sitting.

He didn't need to know. He was happy again. I was happy. *We* were happy. Plus, it was my birthday, and she was definitely not invited.

Why do I keep thinking about this? I don't know exactly. Probably because I had control over that situation, and I have no control now. None. I can't pretend she's ignoring him because we've seen her, and it was clear she wasn't.

If she has the same one, I know the number isn't blocked anymore, because we both got new numbers when we got on the same phone plan.

I don't know if they've talked since we saw her, but I'd be stupid to think they haven't. I don't want to bring her up to him to find out because I don't think I can hide my irritation this time.

So here we stay. In purgatory. One where I probably care too much, and he doesn't seem to care at all.

CHAPTER TWENTY-SIX

Jimmy

Every minute of the day that I spend away from her, I spend wishing I were with her.

Being at work made me think of her. Being at home made me want to be at work, able to think about her in peace.

So, I work on-site as much as I can. It makes the time pass faster because things at home aren't great anyway. Becca and I have not been getting along. It isn't the first time we've gone through a phase like this, but it is the first time I've had something else that made me happy, something to escape to. Becca's mood will eventually pass, but mine? I don't know this time.

It's a good thing that Autumn's hospital is more than five minutes away, or I'd be there every day. I just need her close to me at all times. My life now revolves around her.

I wish we could have more. We've spent the summer confined within a car or the same four ugly walls. I want to be able to enjoy the rest of August with her, and every month after that.

But how do I get us there? Do I just end things with Becca now since we barely speak anyway? But what will that look like? Will I move out? Will she leave? She would never leave that house.

Even then, where would that leave me and Autumn? I'm sure plenty of people would not be happy about it, and I wouldn't want her to take all the blame. Would we keep it a secret a little bit longer? But then, how long?

It's all too much. Every time I try to think about it, I resort to just enjoying where we are right now and checking when the next time I'm going to see her is. *Carpe Diem, right?*

The front door opens and shuts. *Who is that?* I walk down the hallway to see Becca in the living room. She's not supposed to be home.

"Why are you still here?" she asks.

"Why are *you* here?" I rebuttal.

She looks surprised. "I forgot my laptop charger. Your turn."

"I'm working late today." I lie. "I have a meeting at 6:30 p.m."

"On a Friday night?" her tone accusatory.

"Yes."

"Lovely, so I take it you won't be home for dinner?"

"No"

She rolls her eyes and laughs. "K. Thanks for letting me know. Have a great day." Then she slams the door behind her.

I do have a meeting, but it doesn't have anything to do with work. I have a date. Autumn has the night off and suggested getting together for dinner instead of lunch. It doesn't make much of a difference, but if it makes her happy, I'll agree. I might actually sacrifice one of my limbs if it makes her smile.

Since she wants to switch it up, I'll go with it. I get to the room early and do a little rearranging. This room actually has a table, and I put it in the middle of the room instead of up against the wall. I lay the tablecloth across it, then place candles on top. I hate that I can't bring her on a real date, so I'll just bring one to her.

The food is delivered right before she shows up, so it gives me time to lay out the finishing touches. The red tablecloth goes perfectly with the rose-scented candles, her favorite.

I know her knock when I hear it, so I answer the door without hesitation. She looks flawless as usual, but I notice she has makeup on tonight, which is not usual. As soon as the door is shut, she jumps into my arms. It's only been twenty-four hours since I last felt her lips, but it feels like forever.

Her eyes grow as I lead her into view of our dinner. "You did all this?"

"Just for you," I say as I pull her back into my arms.

We eat right away, while the food is still warm. She tells me about her week and about one of her staff that gets on her nerves. I love watching her talk. She is so expressive and animated; you could never be bored having a conversation with her. She tells me about seeing her mom this morning and her new idea of getting a puppy because the house is just *'so quiet.'* She wonders what she did for the last ten years to survive the quiet she keeps talking about.

Once our food is gone, we get comfortably undressed and climb into bed. I hand her the remote, and she puts a movie on. She lays her head on my chest and the rest of her against me, her right leg resting on mine. We lay like this the entirety of the movie, although I don't think she watches any of it. Ten minutes into *Captain Marvel*, I hear her snore.

But I don't care. I've debated the thought a few times, but these days may actually be my favorite. The times when *most of* our clothes stay on, and we just enjoy each other's company. I relish the times I get to soak in the feeling of her body weight resting on mine, inhaling the smell of her hair with every breath.

I know I'll regret not taking the rest of our clothes off when I don't see her again for three days, but right now, in this moment, holding her while she sleeps feels like I'm exactly where I'm supposed to be.

CHAPTER TWENTY-SEVEN

Autumn

While I've enjoyed this summer more than any other summer, I've started to wonder what the future holds and what it could look like.

What it could look like in a reality where Jimmy wasn't married anymore. A smile grows on my face as I imagine a morning like the first time he woke up at my place.

I wake up to him snoring next to me. I throw on his shirt, make us coffee, and he joins me in the kitchen shirtless, because I'm wearing his.

We enjoy the coffee leisurely on the balcony, then he showers and gets ready for work. He kisses me, and I tell him to have a good day on his way out the door.

Because our shifts are not the same, some days he brings me dinner to work, and we eat together during my break. Not hiding in the car, or beneath the rain, but at a table while people walk by and don't think anything different about a happy couple eating together.

And really, would anyone be surprised if we ended up together? Would everyone hate me for breaking them up, or would they understand, given our past? I never saw myself believing in fate until now, but I know that's what this is.

During the times when we were just lying in the hotel talking, he updated me on his family. He told me that they regularly get together with his brother Will and his wife

Chelsey. They schedule outings or dinners with them once or twice a month because they moved two hours north a year ago. He says Becca and Chelsey are really close, but I remember how much his family loved me and how much I loved them, too.

Even though they did then, would they still? And would they welcome me back this way? Or would they wish I had never shown up? I don't know his brother's wife, but would she eventually get over me taking that spot at the dinner table? Or would this end up putting more distance in his and his brother's relationship?

Plus, Jimmy and Becca don't have kids. It could be a clean break for everyone. I will accept my villain status, the one who ruined everything, but then everyone can move on, including us.

But it's also because I've started to fantasize about all of this that I've realized I can't avoid the reality we are in. I have to face it head-on. He deserves to be happy. I deserve to be happy. And I am, but I deserve to be happy and not hide it. I don't deserve to be a secret.

With fate continuously on our side, we get the chance to spend the night together again, since Becca is attending a conference in DC. He is coming to stay at my place, so I plan to lay it all out on the table tonight. I may not be strong enough to stay away from him, but I *am* finally brave enough to say all of the hard things and ask the hard questions. *I think.*

At about 6 p.m., he walks right into my apartment. He lets himself in, carrying our dinner, and walks straight to me for a kiss, like he belongs here, and I love it.

We take our spot on the couch and eat while we catch up on the week. He sits facing forward, and I lay my legs across his lap. He doesn't even mind that my feet are near him while he eats. I love that too.

Once our food is gone, I turn the opposite direction and lean into him, covering us both up with a blanket. He puts on our *secret* favorite nonsense TV show, 90 Day Fiancé, but we barely make it ten minutes into the episode before my courage finally takes over.

"I have to ask you something."

"Anything," he says.

"What do you see in the future?"

"The future?"

"Yeah. Like with me."

He sits up straight, causing me to tense. I sit up too and turn back around to face him. "Well, I hope you're not planning on running away again."

I shake my head. "That's not what I mean."

He reaches forward to slide the strap of my tank off my shoulder. 'Well, in the near future I see…"

I cut him off and back away. "Come on. I'm being serious."

"About what?" He asks with frustration in his voice.

"Seriously?" I snap unexpectedly. "About us."

"Us?"

Now I reciprocate his frustration because all he's doing is repeating my questions.

"Yes, Jimmy. Us. This. Whatever *this* is." I move my hand back and forth between the two of us. "We've been sneaking around for three months now. You can't possibly expect to just do this forever."

He sighs. "Of course, I see a future with us."

"But do you want to be with me or just sleep with me?" I can't believe I finally said it. He takes a second and rolls his eyes, but then responds.

"Autumn, you've been my whole life. As long as you want to be, you are my future."

Now I roll my eyes as I realize I am going to have to be even more blunt than that. He can't be this stupid. "Yeah, but how Jimmy? I didn't move back here to have the best part of my life a secret. I want to be *with* you, but you are married. I love you too much to keep ignoring that."

We both sit silent as we absorb what I just said. I didn't even realize it was coming until it did. Then he smiles.

"I love you too." He says, "I always have. I'm sorry I didn't say it before, and now we're here, but I'll fix it. I don't want to lose you again."

I feel the doe-eyed look creep across my face as I listen to him say everything I've always wanted him to.

"Fix it?" I ask.

"Yes. It's you, baby, it's always been you. I just need to figure it all out."

He's never called me baby before, and he just did it so effortlessly. My whole body feels like a puddle of mush, and I take the bait. He reels my spineless frame into him, and there's no more talking.

I fall for it hook, line, and sinker, willfully ignoring the feeling in my stomach telling me that this conversation didn't change anything.

CHAPTER TWENTY-EIGHT

Jimmy

What is with you lately? Becca barks.

"What are you talking about?" I snap back.

I look over at her sitting on the loveseat. She throws her hands up. "What am I talking about? *This* Jimmy! It's like you're not even here."

"I am here," I argue, "I'm just watching TV right now."

She jumps up. "Oh my God. See. You don't even get it. It's not just about right this second."

"Then what is it about? What do you want me to say?"

She shakes her head. "I don't know. Something? Anything? I don't know what's happened to you recently, but you are not yourself. Do you remember anything I've said to you since you sat down on that couch?"

Realizing I don't, I give her the apology she's looking for. "No, I don't. I'm sorry. I just have a lot going on at the moment." *Not a lie.*

But to my surprise, she gets angrier. "Like WHAT?! I'm assuming work? Because it's not me. It's not your mom. Because I'M taking care of her. I just gave you an update on her, and you didn't hear a damn word I said."

"Yes, with work actually. We have a manager on maternity leave at one location, renovations happening at another, and potentially firing a manager at another." I yell as I jump up. "But never mind. Just forget it!" My stomps echo up the staircase as I storm to the office.

I hear her continuing, but I slam the door and go back to the message I got a few minutes ago.

I'm busy tomorrow.

Busy tomorrow? Tomorrow is Tuesday. We always meet on Tuesdays. I write back.

You're not busy. You're never busy on Tuesdays.

She responds quickly. But her quickness doesn't seem to be from excitement anymore.

Yeah, well I am now.

Okay. What is your problem right now?

I roll my eyes, getting angrier. Once again, she responds right away.

I don't have a problem. I'm sure you could find something else to do. Like work.

Then she sends a separate one.

Maybe your wife wants to do something with you.

I smack the phone down on the bed and take two deep breaths in my hands, my temper rising.

The last couple of days have been different with her. I thought the night we got to spend together went great. She asked about the future, we talked about it, then had a great evening, *and* the next day.

But then with each day that's passed, she's gotten more like this. What did she expect me to do? Just come home and announce that I am leaving the next day? It's not that simple. We have this house, we have our vehicles, we have our pets, and plenty of other things that are going to need to be sorted out.

I don't understand her lack of patience with the situation, especially when I am giving her everything I can right now.

I'm coming to see you.

Immediately, I get:

No, you're not.

I ignore her protest. It's almost her break time. I get up and grab my shoes just as Becca comes around the corner.

"Where are you going? Dinner is done."

"I have to take care of something."

She doesn't even respond, just rolls her eyes and storms away.

It only takes me fifteen minutes to get to the hospital, and her break is in ten. I find her car and then sit on the curb to wait. Twelve minutes after I arrive, she comes around the corner and jumps, startled to see me.

"God, you scared the crap out of me. What are you doing here?"

"Because we obviously need to talk," I say as I stand up.

"About what? You can't wrap your head around the idea that I may have plans that don't revolve around you?" she says back coldly.

"No. See. This is what I'm talking about. Why are you being like this?"

"Like what?"

At this point, I know she's just playing dumb to piss me off. I throw my hands up. "You know what, never mind. I don't know what happened to you, but you're being impossible all of a sudden."

She raises her voice. "You don't know what happened to me?" She laughs. "That's funny because I told you EXACTLY what happened. YOU happened. YOU made me like this. I am sick of being used as a toy when you're bored. I'm not a dumb teenager anymore!" She yells that last part.

"I am TRYING," I respond loudly through my gritted teeth, then bring my volume down, "Would you stop yelling, please?"

She rolls her eyes. "Oh, I'm sorry, am I being too loud? God forbid anyone find out. Wouldn't want your wife to know, right? Then what? She'd be screaming at you, too, right? Yet you're still asking me what my problem is." She laughs again, shaking her head as she turns back to the car, fumbling with her keys. "Maybe she should be. Maybe if she were screaming like me, you'd actually listen to her."

I grab her arm to stop her from opening the car door. "Okay. I'm SORRY." I turn her around to face me and see that she's crying. "Baby, I am trying, I promise. Please hear me." I pause, then say the three words we finally shared the other day. I say them slowly, so she hears each one. "I. Love. You."

She avoids my eye contact, so I lift her chin, making her look right at me. Her eyes finally lock on mine, and we stare at each other for a few seconds. "I don't want to keep doing this, Jimmy. I can't. I'm done sneaking around. This should've never started in the first place, and we're going nowhere. I can't do it anymore." She wipes her cheek. "I can't love you and not be with you."

"I know, I know. Just please see me tomorrow." I plead as I wipe a tear from her other cheek with my thumb.

Her eyes dart away again, looking back at the ground. Her foot is tapping anxiously. I keep talking. "This is a lot for me too, and being with you makes nothing else matter." She continues to stare at her tapping foot until finally mumbling, "Ok."

"Yes? Thank God." A deep exhale escapes my lungs.

She looks up and tries not to smile, so I kiss her. "Sorry for taking almost your whole break," I say as we lean our foreheads together. "See you tomorrow?"

She nods, and I grab her face with both hands for one last deep, reassuring kiss before heading back to my car.

CHAPTER TWENTY-NINE

Becca

I'm already in the shower when I hear him get home.

He doesn't say anything, but I'm not surprised. I am surprised, though, when I get out and realize he's already gone to bed. Not being able to have a full conversation is one thing, but not even saying goodnight?

I get myself dressed and try not to wake him. It's not like he's going to want to talk anyway. I go down to the kitchen to see the dinner that I left out for him still sitting there. Did he even notice that I did that, despite how he acted towards me, and then stormed out? At this point, does it even matter? Whatever is bothering him, he's obviously not going to tell me. If I do try, he shuts me out.

I scrape the food into the trash and begrudgingly wash the dishes as I dry my hands, my phone rings. *Izzy?* At almost 10 p.m. Confused, I answer.

"Hello?"

"Becca?"

"Yeah, What's up?"

"Uhm, I don't know how to tell you this."

I roll my eyes, not in the mood for her typical gossip and dramatics. "What is it, Izzy?"

"I saw Jimmy earlier. At the hospital... With... someone else."

"The hospital?" I question, baffled. "When? With who?"

"I couldn't tell who. I'm just telling you because they were clearly arguing, then kissing."

I don't say anything. My body instantly feels cold. My stomach feels like rocks. The room is being pulled out from under my feet. Suddenly, everything makes sense.

"Autumn," I whisper.

"Becca, I'm so sorry. I don't know if it was her, but it was definitely Jimmy, and I thought you should know."

She started rambling on about how she wasn't sure who, but it was definitely someone, and Dom didn't want her to say anything because he was sure she was confused, but she knew she wasn't. At some point, I tuned out. The last thing I heard was "I'm sorry again, Becca," before I hung up the phone. I didn't care about anything else she had to say.

I walk back up the stairs to the bedroom. Sitting on the foot of the bed, I stare at him sleeping peacefully. His chest rises and falls to a calm cadence, while I can't tell if I'm even breathing or not.

I stare at him for I don't know how long, wondering how long this has been going on; accepting the full scale of the betrayal from the only one I've ever planned a future with. The only one I've ever seen myself with. And despite everything I've convinced myself wasn't that serious before, in this one quiet moment, I accept that it's all been a hoax.

His phone lights up. The voice inside telling me to look returns, and for only the second time ever, I grab it off the nightstand. The screen rattles in my shaky hands, then brightens, and just as I suspected, there's her face in a tiny little circle.

> Sorry for earlier. I love you. See you tomorrow.

I fucking knew it.

The feeling I felt the last time comes back tenfold. The dam holding me together breaks, and I sob. Harder than I've ever sobbed before. To the point that the noises coming out of me are what finally wake him.

He jumps up. "What happened? Becca, what's going on?" He rubs his eyes.

"You just couldn't help yourself, could you?"

"What?"

"Where did you go earlier, Jimmy?"

He squints, "I told you I had to take care of something."

I erupt. "Oh, cut the shit. When did it start? The day we saw her at the restaurant? Or before that?" I gasp and continue, "Oh my God. Was it you? Did she come back for you?" He leans forward, putting his head in his hands, but doesn't say anything. "Yeah. Exactly. I knew it. The moment I saw her back here, I knew I didn't stand a chance."

He looks up and finally speaks. "No, don't say that. It's not like that."

I laugh. "Oh, it's not?" I realize I still have his phone and turn it towards him. "I LOVE YOU?! Are you kidding? Are you really going to try telling me that *she's* just like the others? I'm supposed to believe that it's just like the rest? It's nothing, right? But she loves you? Right?"

I start to lose the sense in my words. I wait for his response, but there isn't one. His silence tells me more than his words can anyway. He sits quietly, staring at the floor to avoid looking at me like the coward I now know he is.

"Exactly." I throw the phone at him and start to pace. "I guess I give you a shred of credit for not trying to convince me that you didn't sleep with her like the others."

I wait for his response, naively still holding on to hope that he didn't actually do this, but still, he doesn't even gather the nerve to look at me. I shake my head in disgust and walk towards the closet, grabbing his suitcase. He jumps up and finally tries to talk.

"Becca, just listen."

I cut him off. "You know what, Jimmy? No. I don't think I want to. All the times we've done this over stupid shit, all the other times I've ignored Izzy because she's usually so full of everybody else's business that she can't see straight, all the times you've told me *'it's nothing,'* and I listened. I convinced myself that you truly did love me, despite sometimes feeling like you didn't. I convinced myself that even though the flirty conversations were wrong, you could never *actually* do that to me. I really thought you could never cross that line. But now I know you have. And quite frankly, I don't have the stomach to hear you admit it or hear any excuses or a bullshit *'explanation.'* Just leave."

He stares at me, confused. Like, I didn't just make myself clear.

"Right now?" He asks.

I fold my arms. "Yes, right now. Get out." I kick the suitcase in his direction for dramatic effect, then turn around to go downstairs and cry alone.

I plop down on the couch, but don't cry like I expect to. The tears have dried, and instead, my leg is bouncing a million miles a minute. I realize I'm biting my nails when he walks past the living room with his bag. He pauses near the front door and looks at me, but I don't say anything.

I just get up and walk past him, making it clear that I have nothing left to say

CHAPTER THIRTY

Autumn

What I did *not* expect on Tuesday was to wake up to messages from multiple people, BUT Jimmy.
Kory.

Hey, I heard some shit... Call me!!

Someone we went to school with.

Should've stayed where you were.

Morgan.

You okay? Call me if you want.

Someone else from school.

Aren't we a little old to still be stealing boyfriends?

I felt a few different things. A sting of pain from the truth behind the harsh messages. But then there was relief. Relief that Jimmy had obviously finally done something. But there was also surprise. Surprise that he hadn't said anything about it, and I still hadn't heard from him. I figured plenty was going on to keep him distracted, so I tried calling, but no answer.

I immediately sent him a good morning text when I woke up, like I always do, before I even read the other messages. But still no response. It's 10 a.m. and we usually get to the hotel around 11 a.m., so I send another asking if everything is okay, but again no response.

Now I'm frustrated because why isn't he responding to or answering my calls? I hope that he just wants to tell me in person, so I jump in the shower. I start the water, eager for this meeting, hoping it is the last secret one.

While rinsing my hair, I hear a text interrupt *Lover* playing on YouTube. Ms. Swift couldn't have released a better album at a better time. But I finish the song and my shower before checking it. Once I'm finally out, I rub the steam off the screen, and I see that the message is from him. *Thank God.*

But then I read it.

Raincheck. I'm at my brother's.

Frustration turns to confusion. I text back.

What? Why? After yesterday?

He writes back.

Yeah, long story.

Confusion now turns to anger.

No. Call me. NOW.

After all that crying and whining about ME cancelling and having an attitude with him? And him showing up at my work even though I told him not to? Now I'm just supposed to be okay with *'raincheck'* and *'long story'*? No.

My message is still sitting on read, so I call him again anyway.

"Hello." He answers, sounding muffled and as irritated as I am.

"Hello? What is going on, Jimmy? Why am I getting messages about us from random people? And why are you at your brother's?

I hear him sigh. "Becca knows about us and kicked me out last night after I got back from the hospital."

"Okay? So why didn't you come here? Why did you go two hours away?"

"It's complicated."

His tone stings me in a way I can't explain. Then I realize exactly what he said and laugh. Why? I'm not really sure.

"Wait, she kicked you out? You didn't tell her and leave by choice?" He sighs again. Which is really just irritating me more.

"No. Apparently, someone saw us at the hospital and told her. She was really upset."

I push my fingertips into my forehead, exerting my frustration. "Well, I mean, I understand that she would be, but wasn't this the goal? I don't understand why you went all the way out there instead of just coming here?"

"I told you it's complicated."

Now anger turns to fury.

"No, it's NOT actually. You had a choice. Like, literally had the opportunity to choose me, and you still can't. All that begging and promising you did to me yesterday, and for what? Now you're the one bailing when we don't even have to hide anymore?"

He sighs for a third time. "I know. I'm sorry. I know how crazy this sounds. I just need to figure everything out."

I laugh again. "No. I have been listening to you *'needing to figure it out'* for months now, Jimmy. Clearly, you have.

This is nothing but an affair, and I've been dumb enough to expect more out of you when I shouldn't."

He clears his throat. "Stop, you know it's not."

"Clearly it is."

"Okay." He takes a breath. "Can you meet me out this way? Like maybe halfway? So we can talk in person?"

I think in silence for a minute. He knows I'm not actually busy. My plans for today were with him. Which HE begged me not to cancel.

"Fine," I finally respond. "Send me an address."

I towel dry my hair, throw some clothes on then head right out the door. Roughly an hour later, I pull into a Denny's parking lot. I see him standing by his car, and instead of waiting for me to get out and walk in together, he comes to me and gets in the passenger seat.

He leans in for a quick kiss as I hoped he would, and leans his forehead against mine for a quiet, comforting moment. Just being next to him has me feeling slightly relieved, so I sit there enjoying it before starting the conversation.

"Hi," I say, which I've said hundreds of times at this point, but it suddenly feels awkward.

"I'm sorry about all this." He says.

"Me too"

Then it's quiet again.

"So what happens now?" I ask.

He sits up and stares forward out the window, then responds quietly. "I don't know."

My eyes immediately start filling with anger. "Then why am I here?" The first tears fall.

"Baby, please don't."

I cut him off. "You know what? Stop doing that. Quit calling me baby. Just stop. If you've meant anything you've said to me, your answer would be easy, and it sure as hell wouldn't be *'I don't know.'*"

He raises his voice and hits the car door. "None of this is easy! You have no idea what this is like for me."

I fire back, loud and not caring who may hear now. "FOR YOU?! For you? Look at me. Look at what a freaking mess you made me! I'm sitting in a parking lot crying like an idiot over someone who doesn't even want to be with me."

"That's not true, and you know it! We wouldn't be in this mess if I didn't want to be with you." He argues.

"Then why can't you say you'll be with me now?" He doesn't answer, and I shake my head. "No. See, we're in this mess because you wanted to have an affair. Just like every other man in the world, you wanted to have your cake and eat it too, and now it isn't fun anymore."

He finally lowers his voice. "I wouldn't have had an affair if I didn't want to be with you. What kind of a person do you really think I am?"

"I don't know. If that's true, why can't you prove it? We have the chance to be together, and you still won't just DO it. All you have for me is more '*I don't know.*'"

Now I sit straight and stare forward. He reaches over and puts his hand on mine.

"Listen, this just isn't how I thought it would happen. I thought the whole thing WOULD be easier. But she looked… so… broken. I wasn't expecting to feel the way I did."

I pull my hands away, and my angry tears turn into frustrated laughs. "And me?" I wipe the wetness from my cheeks. "What am I? This doesn't look broken to you?" He doesn't say anything, so I keep going. "Guess not. She gets to be broken, and I'm just a fool who fell for it all right?"

He finally takes a breath to say something, but I stop him.

"Get out of my car."

"Baby." He pleads.

I put my hand up. "I said, get out. I can't do this anymore, Jimmy. You either want me or you don't. It's pretty simple."

"Baby," he whispers one more time.

"Please go. I have to work." I whisper as I start losing strength.

He doesn't say anything else, and seconds later, the sound of the car door slamming shut makes me jump, even though I knew it was coming.

CHAPTER THIRTY-TWO

Jimmy

Autumn wants more, and Becca wants less.

Sounds simple, but then there's me. I have no idea what I want, and neither of them will talk to me at the moment.

I want to talk to Becca, but she won't reply to a single thing. If she wants nothing to do with me, why can't she just tell me? And if that's the case, what does she expect? Even if staying apart means we're going to have to talk and sort out how this is all going to work. But she won't tell me anything, and I don't know what to do with that.

Then there's Autumn, who told me exactly how she feels. I don't think I've ever seen her as upset as I did that day, and I know I don't ever want to see her like that again. There is a part of me that has always hurt when she hurts, and I can't handle seeing her cry.

But I can't give her what she wants until I talk to Becca. I know whatever happens with us, it will be much harder if she finally calls and I'm with her. I just can't further things with Autumn until it's really over with Becca.

But is it over with Becca? And why does that thought bother me now, too?

Maybe I shouldn't have let Autumn leave like that back then. Thinking back to the last night on her porch, I know I should've begged her to stay, instead of being a dumb, prideful, nineteen-year-old boy. One who just assumed she'd always be there no matter what.

But I didn't, so now I have to consider Becca's feelings when I consider Autumn's. And my own. I can't figure out a way to do that in a way that works out for all of us.

Maybe I shouldn't have jumped into a relationship with Becca when I did. But she was smart and determined, and once upon a time, she made me laugh, and I was done being angry at Autumn for leaving.

Those traits made her a great partner, and I knew she'd be a good wife. She'd be damn near perfect if she weren't so jealous. I could deal with her need to keep up with the Joneses, but she's far more anti-social than me and that's always been a struggle. I've also wondered if that plays a part in her jealousy, too. I like to be out and about, and I like to talk to people. She doesn't. I've never been able to figure out if she is jealous because she's insecure, or if she's insecure because she's jealous.

That's also the biggest difference between her and Autumn. There was never a question about Autumn being by my side, because her personality mirrored mine. She loved to do things and have fun. Most of the time, I didn't even have to tell her where we were going. She didn't ask me a hundred questions about where it was, why we were going, or who would be there. She didn't care about any of it if we were together.

I've also never known Autumn to have a problem with anyone, anywhere *until now*. Becca finds something wrong with just about everyone she meets.

That's why I didn't understand why she wanted to go to her reunion. She doesn't like any of those people. She didn't even like Chelsey at first, but at some point, they became real friends, and now I have to control my temper when I hear her talking about Autumn.

Naturally, she has nothing nice to say and doesn't care that I hear it either. It's clear whose side she's on, and she only tolerates my presence because of my brother.

But it infuriates me. And I know if I get defensive with her, that will only make it worse. She'll run right to Becca and twist my words into a pretzel shaped just right to piss her off.

So I don't. But I want to defend Autumn because she doesn't deserve what Chelsey says about her. None of it is true. She's not a bad person, and even Becca should know that.

But I miss her. Each time my phone rings, I hope it's Autumn. The cold shoulder from Becca irritates me, but from Autumn it hurts. So, despite everything I just thought a few minutes ago, I decide to try again.

> Hey.

That's all I send. I don't know exactly what to say. Do I beg, *'please stop ignoring me?'* A message beeps.

> Hi.

Well… It's progress. My chest feels lighter, so I don't beat around the bush.

> I miss you.

She comes back.

> I bet you do.

That stings. *Is she still mad? Is she being sarcastic?* Then she sends another one.

> Cuz I miss you too.

Relief escapes my lungs.

I need to see you.

I tell her. She responds with the only three words I need to hear.

I'm off today.

My finger slides a sweaty wave of hair behind her ear as we lie in her bed, yet to untangle ourselves from the sheet. She's lying on her back, half covered, and I'm leaning on my elbow, lost in her face as usual, when she looks up at me and smiles.

"I really did miss you." She says breathlessly.

I smile back and kiss her. "I really did miss you, too." I kiss her again.

"I thought you hated me, you know." She says quietly.

I jump up with a scoff. "Hated you? Why would you think that?"

She looks down shyly. "When you didn't call me back. I thought that was your way of telling me you hated me for leaving."

"Call you back? When?"

She squints at me and looks as confused as I feel. "Around Christmas, the first year I was gone. I came home for break and called, then texted."

My shoulders slump forward. All this time, I wondered why she never called, but she did. How did I not know? "Autumn. I had no idea. I have never seen anything from you. I promise I would've called you back immediately if I'd known you reached out." Both of us are quiet for a minute. "Why didn't you try again?"

She shrugs, still looking down. "Like I said, I figured that was your way of showing me how it felt."

Her eyes peek up at me, and they're filled with sadness. I don't like it.

"I could never ignore you even if I tried. Not then, not now, not ever, baby."

She smiles and reaches her arm out, pulling me into her chest. We lay there in silence, and I wonder if she's wrestling with the same emotions that I am.

I am happy and relieved to know she called. Us not speaking all that time confused me the most. I would've given anything to hear from her again. But I am also upset because how did I have no clue? Hearing from her probably would've changed my whole future.

"What did your text say?" I ask.

"I don't remember exactly. Something like I miss you. Just wanted to talk, call me if you want to. So when you didn't, I figured that was you saying you didn't want to."

The way I would've dropped everything if I saw her say she missed me back then...

"Can I confess something, too?" I ask.

"Depends on what it is."

We both laugh. "That day we saw each other after you first moved back? At the diner?"

"Yeah?" She squints, playing with a strand of hair.

"That wasn't an accident. I heard you were back and hoped you would be there."

Her mouth falls open with surprise, but she doesn't say anything. "I was extremely happy to see that I still knew you as well as I thought I did."

"You did not. How did you know what time? Were you stalking me?" she playfully taps my shoulder.

"No, honestly, that was just pure luck. I couldn't believe it."

"I think that's called fate," she says and runs her finger along my arm.

I don't know what else to say, so I don't. I just snuggle tighter into her. She wraps her arm around me, continuing to trace the muscles of my bicep with her finger. I feel the heat from the skin on her chest match the skin on my face. The sound of her heartbeat drowns out the voice that's telling me I can't stay.

But then again, why can't I? I have nowhere else to go and, in this moment, everything feels calm.

I open my eyes to find my face buried in her hair and my arm tightly secured to her. We fell asleep. I try to pull my arm away without waking her, but fail. She rolls over, rubbing her eyes.

"I never nap." She says.

I laugh, knowing this isn't the first time she's fallen asleep with me. "Me either."

"What time is it?" she asks as she pushes herself up to sit.

She doesn't hide herself with the sheet as she runs her fingers through the tangles in her hair.

I turn over to grab my phone off the floor, but the time isn't what catches my attention. It's a text. From Becca.

GO FUCK YOURSELF

Well… Good to know that no progress has been made there. I shake my head, annoyed, but the message also relieves some of the panic I just felt from falling asleep here. Who cares what time it is? I really have nowhere else to be. I drop my phone back down on the floor and roll back over to face Autumn.

"It's after 6:00 p.m.," I say as I lay my head on her thigh.

She puts her hand on my head and starts brushing her fingertips through my hair. It gives me chills. "Wow, we slept for three hours? What time did you get here?"

"Well, I got here around 1:30 p.m., but that's definitely not what time we fell asleep." I squeeze her thigh, knowing she is extremely ticklish, and she hates it. She immediately reacts, laughing but also jumping, trying to wiggle free of my grasp. She continues thrashing about until she's lying back down and now entirely underneath me. I watch her eyes defensively dart from side to side, expecting me to start again, but I don't. "Want to go get some dinner?"

Her eyes grow. "Like, go out somewhere? Together?"

I kiss her forehead. "Yes. You. Me. Food." I kiss her lips. "Together."

I know why she's asking, and I know what this means to her because it's exciting for me, too. This is what we've both been waiting for.

She shoves my shoulder, and I laugh as I dramatically fall onto my back. I keep laughing as she throws the sheet over me and jumps out of the bed, sashaying right to the shower. The smile on my face remains fixed as I stare at the ceiling. Making her happy *really* is my favorite thing to do.

I love it almost as much as I love hearing her sing in the shower.

CHAPTER THIRTY-THREE

Becca

Occasionally, I find myself staring at the half-empty closet.

The bathroom counter and shower shelves are just as bare. I started getting used to the feeling of his absence, but the physical sight of it is harder.

I spent an entire day packing up everything that reminded me of him. I took down every picture, emptied every drawer, and bagged up every pair of shoes, not caring if they were the '*nice*' ones or not. They were all thrown into the same trash bag. That was a good day for me. An angry playlist played loudly in the background as I used it as motivation to erase everything I could. I knew it wouldn't solve the problem, but it made me feel better in the moment.

What else made me feel better? Telling him exactly how angry I was. I still wouldn't respond to any of his attempts at conversation, but every now and then I'd let him know how I really felt. '*Go Fuck Yourself,*' '*Rot in hell,*' and '*You disgust me*' were a few of my favorites.

For about a week, I thought I was getting better. I accepted where we were, learning to live with the looks, and convincing myself that I'd just come out of this the better person. Better than either one of them, at least.

But then I made the mistake of going to do some work at Starbucks. The office had way too much of his stuff in it to pack up, so I just shut the door and pretended the room didn't exist. I thought a change of scenery and expensive coffee would be good for me.

Had I been the only one with the idea that day, it would've been fine, but I wasn't. A few minutes into me minding my business and enjoying the savory aroma of coffee beans, Autumn's best friend walks in, talking on the phone. She was distracted with her conversation and didn't notice me, but after getting her salted caramel iced coffee, she sat just within my ear's range. I could only hear her side of the dialogue, but it was obvious who she was talking to and what they were talking about. The parts that caught my attention the most?

"Well, it's about time that you guys did something besides have sex."

"What movie did you see?"

"Has it been weird for him to be there in the morning when you wake up?"

"He did what?"

"Of course he did. He's going to do all the cute crap he couldn't do before to keep you from changing your mind."

I couldn't take it anymore. All of my executive function skills went right out the window, and impulse took over. As I lunged out of my seat, she saw me and immediately put the phone down.

"You think this shit is cute?" I yelled.

I could tell by her face she had no idea I was sitting just feet away. "Becca." She tried, but I cut her off.

"No. You're just as bad as they are. Never mind, he has a *wife,* right?!"

At that moment, I realized the whole store was quiet. Even the sounds from the coffee machines seemed to be missing. Everyone was staring. "You guys can have each other. All of you!" I grabbed my stuff and stormed out the door.

Now, not only was I the one that they felt sorry for, but I had just turned myself into the one who was losing it. That wasn't how I wanted it. I wanted to be the one with her head held high, while they sulk around, ashamed because they know they're wrong.

He cheated. Everyone knew this. They knew he was in the wrong. He was the bad guy. And her? She was worse. She knew he had a wife, and she did it anyway. But now I was the one screaming in a Starbucks while they were in bed together.

I drove home angrier than I had been the whole time. *How dare they?* The audacity they had to just keep going like they were the ones getting a happy ending. Did he really not care about me at all? He obviously didn't care how this made him look, but did he also not care about how it made me look? Because it made me look pathetic.

I barreled into the house with the thought of burning all his things. At the very least, I was going to put them out in the front yard and let the elements have them.

But that's not what happened.

As soon as I turned into my bedroom and saw all the boxes and garbage bags, I felt my soul finally leave my body. The anger evaporated into tears. I fell straight down and cried for only the second time since I found out. And this time I let it all out, sobs and screams, right there on my knees on our bedroom floor.

I spent so much time being angry that I hadn't let myself be hurt. Hearing that they were actually together now was the real nail in the coffin. This whole thing was real. This was my life now. I was the one whose husband left her for someone else.

I sent one last message and decided that was going to be the last.

> I hope you two are happy now. You deserve each other. <3

I hoped the heart on the end came off as sarcastic as I meant it.

After the Starbucks incident, I started trying to focus on the future, and the first week went fine. I accepted our fate and started thinking about how things would work from here, how we were going to deal with all of the things that have to be dealt with, splitting apart and moving on from each other.

But somewhere in the few weeks that followed, I've found myself not so sure about anything. I'm not sure if I'm still angry. I'm not sure if I'm still sad. I'm not sure which one I'm supposed to be. And mostly, I'm not sure if I miss him or not.

I'm not sure I'm supposed to, but I'm also starting to feel like I'm not sure *not* missing him is possible.

CHAPTER THIRTY-FOUR

Autumn

Everything was great. Not even great. It was perfect.

We went to dinner at a new place that neither of us had been to before. He opened the door for me, and his hand sat securely on my lower back as we walked to our table. He got a T-bone steak with a loaded baked potato and asparagus. I got the parmesan-crusted chicken with risotto and broccoli. It was all delicious.

After dinner, we went to the movies. We saw *The Final Destination*, an obvious choice considering we had seen all the previous ones together. It wasn't nearly as good as any of the others, but with his hand switching between resting on my thigh or pulling me into him, I could have watched anything.

We decided we weren't tired when the movie was over, so we hit the concession stand on the way out and headed for the park. We walked around the pond with our fingers laced together, when we weren't munching on cookie dough bites.

This particular park is between his place and mine, and a very popular spot for anyone in a thirty-mile radius. People from our hometown go there a lot, and they could've been there at the same time as us. Yet, there we were, strolling along the path, hand in hand, as a couple. *Finally.*

Once I couldn't handle the chill anymore, we went back to my place. We got in the shower together, and the rest of the night was a story I'll be keeping to myself.

It was the perfect day and the perfect start to our relationship, until it wasn't…

The next morning, he went back to his brother's and we talked until bed. The day after, the same. But then the next day, when I asked when I could see him again, the excuses began.

After a few days of excuses, the texting slowed. Now two weeks later, I've barely spoken to him. A few texts a day, usually an *'I miss you too'* or *'I love you too,'* but that's it.

I don't know why or what to do about it. I want to ask him. I know I deserve an explanation for the repeated whiplash, but I can't even get a full digital conversation, let alone a face-to-face one.

I can't settle on one emotion that I feel. I'm sad and confused, but then also angry because why does he keep doing this? Nothing is stopping us now. But then I also catch myself trying to be understanding. Divorce is complicated and messy.

I want to be there for him, but maybe he needs to deal with some things on his own, you know, *'figure it out.'*

I also can't help but fear that the confrontation between Kory and Becca may have played a part. The timing is suspicious, but now that she *really* knows, why would he pull away?

No matter what I'm feeling at any given moment, I always resort to being confused, so I try to stay busy. It's hard because I've been avoiding Kory, knowing she will make me talk. The last few times we talked about the subject, she's seemed to be slowly losing patience, especially after the Starbucks incident. I'm not ready to hear the *'I told you so'* tone in her voice, even though she won't say the words.

Forcing myself to avoid her has made shopping really boring again. If I could guarantee she wouldn't bring up Jimmy, I'd much rather have her with me. But instead, I'm here at the store, alone for the first time since I moved home. On the plus side, without her as a distraction, I may have actually remembered everything.

Confident, I head to the self-checkout line, but as I turn the corner, my cart clips the shelf, causing a row of chips to tumble to the floor. They fall right at the feet of the person in front of me, and he bends down to help pick up my mess.

"I'm sorry about that." I blurt out, embarrassed.

"Don't worry about it." He laughs, and I recognize the voice.

He looks up, and when I see the face, I know why I knew the voice. It's Will, Jimmy's brother. "Autumn. Hi."

"Hey," I say back and paint a fake smile, trying to hide everything that I suddenly feel again. They still look exactly alike.

He reciprocates with a kind smile. One you give to someone you've known for a long time, but also one that says he knows everything. Of course he does, that's where Jimmy's been staying.

"How are you?" I ask him.

"I'm good. You?"

I feel the fabrication of my smile fade just a bit. Do I tell him the truth? Does he care? There are so many questions I want to ask him, but I doubt he'll give me any answers, not to mention the grocery store line is probably not the place. "I'm okay," I say instead. "What are you doing around here?"

"I was just stopping on my way home. I went to visit Mom and grab some stuff for Jimmy."

"Oh." I know my face just fell even more by the look on his. He looks around us, then lowers his voice.

"Look, Autumn, I really do hope you're okay. I'm sorry you guys got all mixed up in this."

His comments almost make me cry again right here. Both because I know he's genuine, but also because it sounds like something you'd say to someone who just got dumped. I take a deep breath, determined to fight the tears while I'm in here.

"I'm just really… confused at the moment. But I'll be okay, I think."

He nods and tightens his lips together, checking our surroundings again. Clearly, he doesn't want to be seen on *'my side.'* "Just give him time." He leans in for a quick half-hug. "It was really good to see you." He says before heading to the open register.

Just give him time. I've given him time. I've given him years. How much more am I supposed to give before I finally run out?

The whole encounter rattles me. Scanning and paying for my items is a blur. My mind is racing more than before I came.

As I'm walking to my car, I see Will putting his cart away. Before I can stop myself, I call out his name. I see his shoulders tense, like he was hoping I wouldn't do this, but he turns to face me anyway.

"Why is he ignoring me now?"

He rubs his fingers across his forehead. "I honestly don't know Autumn. I don't know anything he's thinking right now, I promise."

"Did he tell you we spent the weekend together?"

He looks at the ground. "He didn't, but I kind of assumed when he didn't come home."

"All I keep hearing about is time, Will. Time to figure it out. Time, time, time, time. How much time can I give before believing I'm just being strung along?"

"I know. I feel for you. I really do. I meant it when I said I'm sorry."

My fight ends, and the tears start again. They don't fall, but my vision blurs as they gather in my eyes. "I just don't know what to do," I whisper.

He pulls me into a gentle hug. "I'll talk to him." He releases me, resting a hand on each of my shoulders. "But you need to know I won't sway him in one direction or the other. Becca is our family now, but you also don't deserve to be in limbo."

I nod and wipe my eyes. "Thank you, Will. I'm sorry too."

"I know you are kid." He says with a small smile before he turns around and gets in his car.

Once I get mine loaded and started, my playlist picks up where it left off, blaring Cruel Summer. I promptly turn it off, not ready to be reminded how cruel this one seems to have been.

CHAPTER THIRTY-FIVE

Jimmy

New gym, same light problem. Do these places do it on purpose to save on the electric bill?

None of the lights ever works properly. I wonder if they actually had them all functioning at once, if it would all give out and blow.

At this point, that seems to be a good metaphor for my life. I have no idea what I am doing, except that I know I am not *all in* on anything. And I fear that if I do go all in on something, it will all blow up in my face.

I haven't tried to talk to Becca since I learned what that last text was about. I was right. She was definitely even angrier to find out we were still seeing each other. And the fact that she heard it from Kory, Autumn's most reliable source, there was never even a chance at plausible deniability.

But I did love that weekend we shared, so why do I find myself hiding from her? From both of them, right when it starts getting good.

I don't need a shrink to tell me I'm afraid. Becca was right. I'm a coward. Afraid of a divorce? Not so much. Afraid that there was so much electricity between me and Autumn that the whole thing might blow up? Yes.

I run through a few more sets before heading to the locker room. Sitting down on the bench, I stare at the checkered floor, letting my eyes adjust after having stared at the lights for so long.

I know I'm scared. I always have been, yet I do everything in my power not to appear that way. But of course, now I wonder if I hadn't always been scared of how Autumn made me feel, we wouldn't be in this situation now.

It almost always goes back to her prom night, and I remember more details each time I revisit the memory.

After the girls changed out of their lake-soaked dresses, and we out of our sand-smeared dress pants, we all went back down to the beach for a fire and some drinks. We found a soccer ball, and even though none of us actually knew how to play soccer, we started a lawless game.

Running around and kicking a ball in the sand wasn't easy, and at some point, each one of us had fallen at least five times. But the game was filled with laughter, hers the only one I could really hear.

After having that moment watching her in the water earlier, I found myself doing it over and over again. Everything she did made me smile. Everything she said made me laugh.

She had on a T-shirt with little shorts and had taken all of the pins out of her hair. It was big and messy from the wind and running around, but again I caught myself thinking that I had never seen her prettier, maybe even including two hours before, when each strand was neatly secured in place, and she was dressed like Cinderella.

Once she was cold enough to ask to wear my hoodie, I knew the night was about to be over. The fire was dwindling, and she was sitting in the sand, smiling up at me in my clothes and wild hair. I couldn't wait one more second to ask her if she wanted to go to bed.

"With you?" she asked.

"Yeah, come on," I said as I grabbed her hand and led her back into the house without saying goodbye to the rest of the party.

We each took turns in the shower, rinsing as much of the sand away as possible. I knew my mind was made up hours ago, but as I watched her work the brush through her wet hair, I knew exactly what I wanted. I wanted her, but not just to sleep with her. I wanted to hold her. I wanted to kiss her.

I didn't wait until she was done untangling her hair. I slowly grabbed the brush from her hand, and she looked up at me like the characters in every romantic movie she's ever made me watch. I grabbed her hand and pulled her up, and neither of us said anything. It was obvious we were on the same page.

I tucked a piece of hair behind her ear and went in for a kiss. I don't think that kiss even ended until we were wrapped up together under the sheets, too tired to even say good night before falling asleep.

At some point, I woke up to her tossing and turning. Once she re-settled, she mumbled "I love you" in her sleep.

It made me smile, and then it didn't. Although I wanted to say it back, that was the first time my fear showed its ugly head. I panicked and snuck out of the room to sit on the deck and think for a minute.

She was my best friend, and I had a feeling I loved her too. But everyone always said not to date your best friend because one of you will be hurt and the friendship will be over. So I couldn't admit to myself that I was in love with her. I wouldn't. I couldn't risk giving her up in any sense.

So, I sat out there and thought about all the ways it could go wrong, not once thinking about how it could possibly go right.

CHAPTER THIRTY-SIX

Autumn

Moms are so special. They have a superpower that should really be studied more.

I thought I was getting away with it the last couple of months, pretending everything is good. Pretending nothing is wrong. But it isn't good, something *is* wrong, and the more time that passes, the more upset I get. And here she sits on the porch staring at me, waiting for me to tell her the truth.

"I know when something is wrong with my only child." She insists.

I stare across the yard, folding my cardigan tightly across my chest. Has October finally brought the cold, or do I just have the anxious chills? I don't want to admit any of this to my mom, of all people, but I'm not coming up with a lie quick enough. She taps her fingers on the patio chair, impatient.

"I don't really want to tell you, Mom. I messed up."

She scoffs. "Unless you hid a body in my house without my permission, I don't care what you did. Fess up."

I let out a tiny laugh, realizing she's gone insane. "It's Jimmy."

"Jimmy? Your friend Jimmy? What's the matter?"

I cock my head to the side and glare at her, hoping she'll read it in my eyes. I still can't say it out loud. She stares back for a few seconds until her eyes finally expand with realization.

"Oh." She says, followed by a louder, more pronounced "OH!" confirming she put the gist of it together.

"Yeah" is all I can say as I continue to stare into the yard.

"Hmph," she starts. "Did you guys not try this enough in high school?"

"MOM!" I exclaim.

I can't believe she said that. I can't believe she thought that. I'm too stunned to speak, so she does.

"I'm just saying. I thought this was old news." She says, as matter-of-factly as possible.

"How many times do you think we…" I stop and shake my head. "You know what, never mind."

"Honey, stop getting so defensive. I'm your mother. I'm just saying that I wasn't stupid, for one, and that I thought you guys moved past this."

"So did I." *Even though I know I never did.*

"You know this is wrong, right?"

"Yeah, Mom." The roll of my eyes transports me right back to my teenage years on this porch.

"So, what happened?" I look at her, confused. She asks again. "Tell me what happened. How did you get here? I want to hear about it."

I continue to look at her questioningly, but she nods for me to go on. I guess I have no choice but to finally say it out loud after all. I take a deep breath and tell her everything from prom to me leaving, to us reuniting, to Becca finding out, to the last time I saw him, to Becca confronting Kory. She sits quietly for a minute, taking it all in.

"No wonder I got kicked out of my book club."

"MOM!" I yell at her again, but she is laughing.

"Oh, lighten up. I am messing with you. I missed out on years of these conversations with you. Cut me some slack here." She pauses. "I would never join a book club."

We both laugh. I do appreciate her sense of humor now. I don't remember her being this funny before.

"Well…" she starts, "What do you want to happen?"

I'm surprised she asks me this. I expected a lecture about all the reasons I already know I'm wrong. I think for a minute as a tear slides into the corner of my mouth. "I want him to love me, Mom. The way I've always loved him."

She nods, and I wipe the twin of the first tear off my other cheek. "You said that he admitted he loves you too, no?"

"Yeah, he *said* it, but I'm still sitting on this porch crying. It's been two months since it came out, and he still *'doesn't know.'* I haven't seen him in like a month, and we've barely even spoken."

We're both quiet. I continue staring ahead into the yard, watching the squirrels desperately trying to find every last piece of food for winter. They dart in and out of traffic, lucky to make it to the other side. It's the time of year when many of them meet their end by car, too impulsive to watch where they're going. Kind of like what I've done to myself.

I keep talking. "And even that doesn't make sense. The last day we were together was *so* good, Mom. It was the first time we got to be together truly like old times. But better. We were *together*. We didn't have to worry about who knows, because everyone already does. We went out to eat, we went to a movie, and then went for a walk through the park holding hands. It was all so normal, but then practically nothing. Why hasn't he tried to see me again? If he loved me the way I love him, I wouldn't still be alone and waiting."

She nods again. "It sounds like you already know what you need to know."

I look down and swallow the lump in my throat. She keeps talking.

"I hope you get everything you want, honey. I want you to be happy, no matter what that looks like, but this isn't an easy situation. One that doesn't usually work out well for the *'other'* one. I hate to say this, but you need to prepare for the worst."

I nod as I listen, further appreciating the lack of lecturing in this moment.

"I wish you had told me some of this back then." She says.

The tone of her voice changes. It's not light and funny anymore. It's quiet and sad, and suddenly I feel like crap. Not because I just admitted to being in love with a married man, but because I realize that *she* realizes that we lost all that time together over a boy.

I get up and sit on her lap like a kid, pulling her into a hug. "I'm sorry, Mom."

She hugs me back tightly, and I hear her sniffle. Mine echoes hers.

"I'm sorry too. You deserve so much love, Autumn. But you deserve to be loved proudly. Do what you feel you need to do, but please don't forget that."

I honestly don't know what I need to do, nor do I know what to say. I just enjoy this quiet moment as a grown woman crying in my mother's arms.

Eventually, I free my mom from the weight of my body and emotions. We don't talk about it anymore. She moves on to preparing dinner, and I go to my old room. It's finally stayed different, officially no longer *my* room. There's a gaping hole in the middle where my bed used to be. A few boxes I don't recognize have gathered instead, appearing to make this a new storage room.

I go over to the closet and pull out the note box. I don't know why I didn't bring it with me to my apartment. I guess I feel like it belongs here. After planting myself on the floor, I dump them all out on the floor and spread them out, looking for one in particular. One I wrote, disguised on the outside as being from someone else, in case it was ever found. It doesn't take long to find it, two hearts filled in with glitter gel pen. One silver for April, his birthstone, and one red for January, mine.

I probably shouldn't read this right now, but I open it anyway. I'm pretty sure this was the last note I ever wrote, on the morning of my graduation.

Dear Jimmy,

I'm moving. I wanted you to be the first to know. My family's not moving. Just me. I'm not going to Grand Valley. I'm going to the University of Wisconsin. Yes Wisconsin. I'm sorry I didn't tell you before, and I'm sorry for lying for the last few months, but I have decided. I'm going.

I can't go to GV because I don't want to be your friend anymore. I can't be. I think I love you, and I know you don't love me back. I don't think I'm mad at you for that, but I don't want to pretend anymore. And I can't be around you and not be your friend, so I'm leaving.

Actually, I think I am a little mad. Why did you sleep with me after prom if you didn't like me like that? Why you had sex with me is a question in itself, but that's probably an easier answer. But why did you sleep with me? All the space available in the lakehouse, why did you sleep in the bed with me? Why did you wrap your arms around me and hold me until we were asleep? Why did you kiss the back of my neck? Maybe you thought I was sleeping, but you still did it, and I remember.

I felt like it was special, and you just didn't seem to care. Why couldn't you even acknowledge it the next day? I was fine not talking about it that night because it was a long day, and a long night, and we both know I was ready to sleep. But you didn't even say good morning. You didn't even talk to me. You practically acted like I didn't exist.

I don't understand. Then two days later, you were talking about another girl, and I had to pretend it didn't hurt my feelings.

It sucks because you know you are my best friend. You always have been, and I thought you always would be, but I can't anymore.

I'm sorry if I'm the one who messed this up by wanting more, but I do, so I can't be your friend anymore. I probably sound crazy, and now that I'm writing this, I don't even know if I'm going to give it to you. I probably shouldn't.

Anyways. I hope I do because I hope you like me more, too, but I think I'm too scared to find out you definitely don't. I hope you don't hate me for leaving.

Love your best friend,

Autumn.

One lonely tear hits the page. I fold it back up before anymore of the ink smears. I know I never actually planned to give this to him. I wrote it for myself, to remind myself why I was leaving.

The letter reeks of desperate teenage turmoil, yet I still have all the same feelings. I wish I could tell this younger version of me that it got better, that it all worked out, and that she still had her best friend.

But it didn't, and despite her valiant effort, it actually got exponentially worse.

CHAPTER THIRTY-SEVEN

Jimmy

The fall air is finally crisp, but still comfortable.

I sit out on Will's patio, enjoying the fresh air and quiet. It's the first time in a week, maybe a while, that I feel like I can really breathe.

I didn't understand why he moved all the way out here at first. Even after visiting a few times, I still didn't get it. We were always city people. All of our family was there, including our mom, who we just found out is sick.

Living in the middle of nowhere, surrounded by nothing but trees, never sounded appealing to me. But right here, right now, I get it.

I can hear nature, and I don't think I ever have before. Most people probably wouldn't even describe nature as something you can hear, but you can. I can hear the wind through the trees. I can hear animal sounds that are new to me. You can't hear a single person or car. Just air through the trees, rustling leaves, water in the distance, and unidentified animal sounds.

And then there's the colors. The leaves have just begun to change, but you can see why people talk about the *'beauty of fall'* out here. Each tree already has a vast array of golds, reds, oranges, and some greens. I understand now how this could be nice to get used to, especially on days like today.

Not too long after that epiphany, Will joins me at the table and hands me a beer. He knew from the start why I showed up here, even though we haven't really talked about it much. I'm sure Chelsey was one of the first people Becca called, so he probably knew before I finished the drive out here.

Chelsey is exactly why staying here wasn't exactly my first choice, but I just work extra hard to avoid her when she's home, which unfortunately is most of the time.

"You know, I hate to say it, but I had a feeling you'd get yourself into a mess like this." He says.

"What's that supposed to mean?"

He looks at me with raised eyebrows. "You're kidding me, right? The minute you called and told me she was back. I heard it in your voice. Plus, you feeling excited enough to tell me was a red flag too. That first dinner we had after she was here, I knew something was up with you."

I stare off into the trees, listening but not responding. He keeps talking.

"I'm just saying. I'm not judging you, I'm your brother. I've been there since you two met, and I know why you did it. I get it. But now you have to figure out where to go from here. You've hurt them both, and you can only fix it with one of them, and even that's if you're lucky. You don't get to keep both. It's one or neither."

I nod my head, agreeing. "That's the problem." I start "I don't know. I really, *really* think it's Autumn. I am almost sure of it. I wouldn't have just gone out and had an affair with some random girl. I really thought she was my person back then, and when she left, I was lost. Then, when she came back, everything seemed normal again. The only reason I find myself questioning it now is when I think of what everyone else will say, because I know it's wrong. But I also know I love her. I always have. It feels like she is supposed to be in my life. She's been there for everything. Until she wasn't, and then it was Becca. And since it's been Becca, I know we've been through our fair share. She's never stopped supporting me, until now. She won't even speak to me. We haven't had an actual conversation since I left. The only time she says anything is to tell me how much she hates me. Yet I still wish she'd just talk to me."

He nods and takes a drink. "Yeah, I do not envy you."

We both laugh. "Thanks, that's real helpful." I take a drink myself.

"Okay." He starts. "Here's my real advice. Picture your future. Being old and having grandkids. Who do you see with you?"

I roll my eyes. "Autumn asked something similar."

He laughs. "Well, she's never been that dumb." I laugh with him again, and he keeps talking.

"Let me say it like this then. How do you feel when you're with Autumn? Like you're kids again, right? Like you did in High School. When nothing else really mattered? Like you had no cares in the world?" I nod. "You still felt that way because it was an affair. I know you don't want to call it that, but that's what it is. True love or not, you can't deny that part of it was fun because no one knew. It was thrilling. You felt like a kid again because you didn't have the real world attached to it."

I keep listening, and he keeps talking.

"With Becca, you don't feel like a kid, because you're not. You guys have a real adult life together. A good one at that. You both had goals, and you've reached them. With that comes real-world stress and responsibility. Subconsciously, when you look at Autumn, you think of sex and fun, and youth, but when you look at Becca, you think of the mortgage, the house that needs to be kept up on, and the groceries that need to be bought. Life with Becca is definitely not going to be fun and exciting all the time, but it's a good, healthy, stable life for two people not even in their thirties yet."

We both sit in silence, enjoying a couple of sips of beer. I hear what he's saying, and he's right. But I don't feel like it makes it easier. He takes my silence as a cue to keep going.

"What I'm trying to say is if you choose Autumn, things will change. That carefree feeling will go away because eventually, all those real-life stresses will be included in that relationship too. Are you willing to start over with someone else, knowing how great you and Becca are as a team?"

I lean forward with my elbows on my knees. "But see that's the thing." I start. "Yes, we're a great team, but I know Autumn and I are too. We always have been. I really can't picture a future that she's not in. I don't know how to live without her."

"But you do." He argues. "You lived without her for ten years."

"Yes, but she's back, and it feels like she never left. We literally picked up, like, not a day passed. I don't think Becca and I would have even gotten together if Autumn had never left."

"But she did. And you guys did. Is that fair to Becca?"

"No, I guess not, but is it fair to me to stay with someone just because we signed a piece of paper if I love someone more?" I look back down. I couldn't hate myself more right now.

"You're right. It's not fair to any of you, but it's not about being fair at this point. It's a mess you made, so *you* have to clean it up. Do you really love Autumn more? Or do all the memories just make you think you do?"

"I don't know. Sometimes I really do, but then sometimes I really miss Becca. But I can't get past feeling like me and Autumn have a second chance, and I'll regret it if we don't take it."

"Look, I'm not on anyone's side but yours. But the reality is that Becca *is* your wife, and I haven't heard you call her that one time. This isn't a breakup. This is a divorce. And if it's not, she doesn't deserve an unsure husband. You owe her that much. So, my last piece of advice is to make sure you are sure, no matter what you choose. Becca doesn't deserve it, and neither does Autumn, despite her being the *'other woman.'* Maybe make use of this time that Becca is ignoring you to make sure what you have with Autumn is really what you want, or that it is over and done, door closed and locked. You clearly started your relationship with Becca with Autumn's door still propped open. Don't do that again." He pauses for a brief moment. "Also, don't tell my wife I said any of this to you. I will deny all of it."

We laugh, but it's not really funny. I have always hated admitting when he's right, but I think he is this time, too. I still don't know what to do, but I know it's always been Autumn. No matter how hard I tried to forget about her, I never could; I just got used to the absence.

But we have always been connected, and I don't think anything can change that. Since she came back, I'm back to thinking about her everywhere I go. There isn't one thing in this city that doesn't have a memory of her attached to it.

I got used to her absence and pushed her out of my mind, but now that she's back, I don't think I can do it again. I can't stop thinking about her, knowing she could be just minutes away all the time. Every time I go anywhere, I wonder, hope that I will run into her. I don't know how to make that stop.

And I don't think I can be with Becca while always thinking about Autumn.

CHAPTER THIRTY-EIGHT

Autumn

"Ugh, seriously, what is wrong with me?" I whine to Kory as we search for reunion dresses.

It's tomorrow, and naturally, we waited until the very last second. Truthfully, I didn't wait at all. I just didn't plan on going, but as predicted, Kory insisted we '*needed*' this.

"I could name a few things, actually." She jokes. I glare at her. "I'm kidding. Geesh, there's nothing wrong with you. You are in love with him. Always have been. He's a dick. Always has been."

I laugh. "Yeah, well, I'm not innocent. I did this to myself."

"True, but he also could've just left you alone."

I shrug and continue to shuffle through the hangers. I only made it four days ignoring him after her last update. We haven't talked about it much since the confrontation at Starbucks. I hated that she got brought into it. I knew it bothered her, too, even though she wouldn't say it.

"Have you guys been talking still?"

With hesitation, I nod, and she immediately shakes her head in dispute. "No, listen." I start to defend myself. "I just don't like how we ended things. I can't explain it, I just know it's not over."

"That's because it's never been over, and I'm sure it won't ever be until YOU finally say it is. You know I'm always on your side, but come on, Autumn, think about it. Why would he stop sleeping with you if he doesn't actually have to? Obviously, being married to someone else wasn't a reason enough to. I would never think bad of you, and I know how much you wanted this to be it, but I'm going to finally tell you that you're better than this."

That hurts a little. I ignore the part of me saying that she's right and continue looking for something to wear to this reunion, which he told me I should go to.

"But we haven't even slept together in like two months. So, according to your theory, why is he still talking to me?"

"I hardly think a few messages a day count as talking. But either way, I don't like it anymore," she says. "I did hear that Becca is bringing a date, though."

"I heard that too."

"So, is he coming as yours?"

I roll my eyes. "He told me he would '*probably*' come if I did. I don't know what that means, but I guess we'll find out. I still don't really want to, I might as well walk in there with a giant red A on my chest."

She shakes her head, "No. The A is for him; you're wearing this. They're going to stare, so you might as well show up ready for it."

She hands me a long, silver, sequin dress that looks like a disco ball. I groan but don't even argue with her. It's better if I just let her pick, or we'll be here forever.

For full nostalgic value, we get ready at my mom's, and she is just loving it. She snaps all the pictures, the white porch rails and rose bushes returning for their role as the backdrop for all the traditional awkward poses. We let her have this one and go along with it, enjoying the laughter.

Kory has a short black dress on. It is satin with spaghetti straps and most definitely something she would not have been allowed to wear in high school. But it looks amazing on her now, and she is stunning with her dark hair pulled up into a ponytail, with just a few strands left out and hanging by her face.

I went the rare route of curling mine. It has been so long since I had my hair like this, I forgot how much I like it. I think I may do it more often. The long, loose waves hang over my bare shoulders and chest. My dress actually feels very high school era; I could not tell you the last time I wore something strapless. Kory made a good choice, though. The sequins were deceiving; appearing stiff and scratchy, but it is actually very stretchy and comfortable. It is the opposite of hers—long and bright silver to her short and black. As usual, we are the yin to the other's yang.

Once we finally make it to the school, we enter straight through the gym doors, and it's decorated exactly how it would have been back then. Black and red balloons fill every corner of the gym. Tablecloths alternate between black, red, and white, with centerpieces of cardboard cut-outs that say '2009,' 'Go Eagles,' and shapes of eagles themselves. Fake dollar store flowers are mixed throughout, which seems like a weird combination to me, but it works for the occasion.

Our school colors are also represented in the copious amount of streamers that hang from the ceiling. I always wondered how they got them up there. Music from the late 2000s is playing at full volume. All of the faces look vaguely familiar, and they're all starting to mingle and talk.

One of the hallway doors is open, and poster boards line the walls with throwback pictures. I was already worried about the looks I would get from people, and this definitely isn't going to help. If there are pictures of me, he's probably in them too, which means I'm honestly probably not in any.

This 'small town scandal' has been all everyone around here has been talking about, like we're still students at this school. Perfect time for a good ole' high school reunion. But do they actually care enough about it to not include photos of us because Becca will be here? Or do they just like to gossip?

I don't waste time even looking through them; I just want to find out if he's here. Kory made a point yesterday, even if it wasn't the one she intended to make. If Becca has a date, why can't he be here with one? Why should I feel bad about being here with him if she is with someone else? That's what happens when people break up; They see other people.

I can't find him, so we get comfortable at a table chatting with Morgan, Olivia, and a couple of other girls we used to hang out with. During the conversation, I see Becca across the room, and she is, in fact, arm in arm with someone. I don't recognize who it is, but it really doesn't matter. She looks happy. Maybe my subconscious just wants her to be, but she actually looks the part. And if she is happy, Jimmy should be able to be too.

She looks gorgeous tonight. She has a navy blue one-shoulder dress that tightens at the waist before growing into a slightly fuller skirt, and the style is very flattering on her. Her chestnut hair is pulled back in a loose updo, with curls falling throughout. When she turns, I notice a slit in the skirt, all the way up to her thigh. She also came ready to be stared at.

Both she and her date laugh as they talk, and she hugs other people as they walk by. I don't realize I'm still staring until we lock eyes. The happy glow I have been watching instantly turns cold. Her hazel eyes suddenly look black. Neither of us looks away until my emotions take over.

I power walk for the door and stand outside, inhaling the fresh air like I haven't taken a breath in hours. What is happening to me right now? I figured she would be here. Why am I fighting off a panic attack? I start fanning myself with my hands even though it's only fifty-two degrees outside.

Do I finally feel it? The guilt I've been avoiding? I knew what I was doing. I thought about it a million times. I thought about her a million times. But I did it anyways. Maybe it was easy to pretend like she didn't exist when I didn't see her, but she does exist, and she's here, and that is harder to accept than I thought.

Resting my hands on my head, I take a deep breath in, when I hear him say my name. His voice melts away the thoughts piling up in my head. I turn around to see Jimmy walking up in a black suit, looking very much the same as he did the last time we were here.

"Are you okay?" he asks. I see concern in his eyes. I missed them so much.

"I'm okay. Better now. You look nice."

He smiles, then kisses my cheek. "You don't look too bad yourself."

"I didn't think you were actually coming," I confess.

He looks away. "I wasn't sure either, honestly. But I've been doing a lot of sitting around, so getting out sounded nice."

We stand awkwardly in silence until I make another confession. "I'm glad you did. Can I hug you?"

He laughs as he takes me right into his arms and we stand there locked together.

"I miss you," I say.

He hears me and reciprocates, then kisses the top of my head. I don't move. I just enjoy this feeling and his familiar scent. He breaks away and kisses me. It's not explicitly passionate, but rather gentle and intimate.

We stand there with our lips together, savoring every second we've missed. His hand feels so warm on my cheek. He feels it too because he pulls back and rubs my arms.

"Aren't you cold?" I shake my head and lie, never wanting to stop. "Well, let's get in here before you do get cold then." As he says that, he laces his fingers into mine, and now I am beaming.

Tonight is the night we finally make it past this awkward stage of being a secret. We can move on from *'just friends'* to an affair, to a real relationship. The guilt is gone now, because this is his choice. We may not have gone about it the right way, but he wants to be here with me, so here we are.

I squeeze his hand as we walk through the hallways. I see the looks, but none of them matter right now. Kory sees us from across the room, and her eyes widen with a smile. Maybe she'll get back on board. She doesn't really have a choice.

Once across the gym, we sit for a minute at the table. He puts his arm around the back of my chair. I can feel his suit jacket sleeve on my back, and I can't stop smiling. *This is real.* A couple of people stop by to chat, and he doesn't shy away from me; he even kisses me on the cheek once.

Kory comes over and says hi, then a few more join. I am still aware of the ones acting like they will catch cooties if they come near us, but I don't care. Jimmy's friend Dom comes over, and they get lost in their conversation, so I get up to get us drinks.

I know I am the one glowing this time. It's my turn. As hard as it was not to see him lately, I know he needed that space to finally *'figure it out' as much as I hated each time he said that.* But tonight, we are here, and we are enjoying each other's company without having to hide. It's finally *our* turn. I hurry to get back with our drinks because a slow song is on, and I want nothing more than to be back in his arms, in this room, swaying to the music, surrounded by all these people.

I approach him with his drink, but he doesn't turn to grab it, so I nudge his arm. He still doesn't turn towards me, so I follow his gaze to find what is so interesting.

Becca is slow dancing with her date.

I look back at him and realize his whole demeanor has changed. In an instant, so does mine. All the joy that was just beaming out of me? *Gone.* Kory also sees, and her eyes plead with me not to lose it. By the time I look back towards Jimmy, I realize why she is pleading.

He's gone, and once again I'm left standing here by myself, confused.

CHAPTER THIRTY-NINE

Jimmy

I couldn't stay at the reunion.

I one-hundred percent ran away, leaving Autumn, Becca, and her date behind. Seeing Becca with someone else hit me in a way I didn't expect. And I couldn't explain it.

She told me she wasn't going. She said there was no way she would go there when it was all the people who knew how stupid she looked.

I went because my brother was right. I needed to spend time with Autumn to figure out what to do, and in my recent cowardly fashion, I had been avoiding her. I thought it would be nice to be out with her again. Not just in her apartment or a hotel room, where inevitably one thing would lead to another. And since Becca wouldn't be there, I thought it would be the perfect opportunity.

But then I saw Becca for the first time in months, but what felt like years, in the arms of someone else. Everything else went out the window. I can't explain anything, and I know it all sounds insane. She was with someone else because I was with someone else. I was there with someone else, but couldn't stand the sight of her with someone else.

I thought it was Autumn. I really did. I went there to be with her, but then I saw Becca with him, and it was overwhelming. It wasn't how I expected to figure out what I was going to do, but it was.

Autumn texting me asking where I went was another knife to the gut, this time being twisted around. I couldn't face her. I didn't want to tell her why I was upset.

As I drove away from that school, emotions finally punched a hole in my chest for the first time in months. I had to pull over to let them out. I finally knew. I needed to fix things with Becca.

I sat there on the side of the road, exploding emotions that I couldn't sort out. It had been so long since the last time I cried; I know I let out years of it during that time in my car.

I couldn't stop replaying the hurt on her face that night in our bedroom. I couldn't stop replaying the sight of her with someone else and the feeling in my stomach that came with it. I finally knew without a doubt what I was going to do, yet hated myself for it at the same time.

I knew what this was going to do to Autumn. She was right. I should have left her alone. I yelled as loud as I could and hit the steering wheel over and over again.

This was never my intention. I really thought we were meant to be, but now I don't think we are. And I have to tell her that. My best friend. I have to break my best friend, and I know we won't come back from this. The stories I heard way back then, about why you shouldn't date your best friend, the stories that kept me from doing this then; they were all right. We will be ruined. Friendship gone. My heart screams at me, calling me an asshole.

So then why do it? If I knew what this was going to do to both me and Autumn, why couldn't I make another decision? The part of me that hurts when she hurts is already shattered.

My brain knows what I am going to do. I am going to scrape what little bit of integrity I have left off the ground and go to my wife. But even though my mind is made, I'm not sure my heart is going to catch up.

When I make it back to my brother's, I go straight to my room and stay there until I fall asleep. Before I left for the reunion, I told him what my plan was and who I thought I had chosen, and I didn't feel like explaining that it had changed or why it did. I didn't bring it up at all for a few days.

I've been trying to call Becca since the day after the reunion, and she still won't answer. But it's been almost two weeks, so I stoop down to the teenage level of calling her from another number. My brother's house phone. Why they still have one, I don't know, but it works, and I finally hear her voice.

"Becca? It's me."

"What do you want?"

I hear the agitation. "I want to come home. I want *you*."

"Yeah, well, that's not going to happen." She replies sharply.

"Becca, please, I'm sorry. I'm so sorry. I was wrong. You were right about everything. I know this is the worst thing I've ever done, but I want to make it right. Please believe me. Tell me to do anything. Whatever you want. I'll do anything to make it up to you." She doesn't respond, so I keep pleading my case. "Your birthday is this weekend. Let me do something for you."

"I'm going out with friends."

"Let me come with you."

"Definitely not. I am doing this without you."

"Please," I beg. "I miss you."

"I can't do this, Jimmy. Goodbye."

She hangs up, and I slam my fist on the counter. Of all the thoughts I've struggled with lately, not once have I considered her *not wanting* me back. I'm going to have to do everything in my power to get her to change her mind. But with Becca, that is not an easy task. While it may not be easy, I know her and I know what's most important to her. If I can put this back together and rebuild the perfect image she wants us to live, I can win her over.

My phone starts ringing in my pocket. I pull it out to see who is calling.

Autumn.

CHAPTER FORTY

I had to hang up on him, or I might have caved.

I knew it would happen. I knew he would feel like crap seeing me with someone else, which is why I told him I wasn't going.

It was the only time I responded to one of his questions. He asked me if I was still going, and I said most definitely not, even though it was most definitely a lie. That's why Stephen was my date, but that's all he was. All he is. A friend from work, who offered some moral support with a side of pettiness. Plus, I am as far from his type as one could be.

I knew I would need that support when I saw her, especially if they had the nerve to show up together like I suspected. I went in with a plan to ignore her, because I didn't want to get emotional and cause a scene again. I have dealt with more than enough people in my business lately.

I do accept some of the responsibility for that part, though. I was pretty heated that first day and had no shame in telling whoever would listen what he did to me and who he did it with. Plus, I couldn't decide if his being with Autumn was worse than if it had been with some stranger he met at work or something. I felt like it was worse.

I mentally prepared ahead of time to be the bigger person. One thing I was not going to allow to happen was a repeat of Starbucks. But then, actually seeing her reignited so many feelings. Anger, hurt, betrayal, jealousy. I hated her so much, but I still couldn't stop staring at her. She looked beautiful, and that made me hate her more. Watching her contagious smile spread to everyone she walked by just made me feel even smaller.

Then she saw me, and as we stared at each other, I started to see past the façade. There was sadness in her eyes. Was it me? Did she actually care about what she'd done to me? Or was she sad because she ended up there alone, and I didn't?

The look in her eyes got me feeling more strong than small. I held eye contact with her, and it felt like I was saying *'Yup. I'm here and I'm okay.'*

I kept my eyes on her until she ran out the door. Stephen stood watchfully next to me the whole time. He knew what was happening—I'd shown him plenty of pictures—and asked if I was okay once she ran. I confidently told him I was good.

After seeing her alone, I thought Jimmy hadn't had the nerve to show up. But when she came back into the room, there he was, holding her hand with a smile on his face. Her smile was back, too, and I realized she didn't give a shit about what she did to me. She *was* sad because he wasn't there. Now there they were. The sight took away some of the strength I had just gained.

Feeling like I was going to pass out, I sat down with my head resting in my hands. Stephen followed me and, as the saint he is, convinced me not to do that. Not to hide and let them ruin my night. I had just as much right to have a good time as they did. After all, Jimmy was the one who initially pointed out that this was my reunion, not his.

By the time I collected myself, a slow song had come on. Stephen further insisted that I not let them win and to get up and join him on the dance floor. I conceded but buried my face in his chest to avoid the rest of the guests looking at me.

"Mayday Mayday," he whispered. "Don't look now, but he sees us. He definitely sees us."

I didn't say anything back, just waited until our slow sway circled me to face that direction. He was staring alright, as Autumn stared at him. She looked at him, then at us, then back at him. The glow that appeared when he did was gone. His eyes were angry, and the sadness in hers had returned. I should've felt bad, but I didn't.

So, I wasn't at all surprised he started calling me almost immediately. But I don't know what he expects me to do. Or what I even want to do. Of course, I still love him. I've tried not to. I've tried to hate him, but I can't. I only hate her.

It did feel strange to finally see him again. I knew then that despite my anger, I really did miss him, but I still can't bring myself to talk to him. How can I let this go?

We went from young college kids to successful adults, and we did it together. I fell for him immediately, and I didn't know for a long time if he felt the same. I also knew I would love him forever. So even with the fear of being hurt eventually, I still went all in.

He was the only reason I stayed together when my dad died. If it wasn't for Jimmy, I would've thrown all that schoolwork away and never looked back. But he was there, empathetically by my side the whole time, and helped me both heal and stay on track, which was normally my job.

Now here I am. I feel like I don't know him at all anymore. And I'm trying to get over the worst imaginable thing a wife can.

I knew he'd come back, but I'm also well aware that I am not actually the *'only one'* for him. I never have been, and we can't hide from that anymore. That's why I finally decided that it *is* worse that it is her versus a stranger.

I know he loves her. I know deep down he does, and as much as I hate her, I know she loves him too. Nothing I can do will change those feelings. Can I live with that?

Can anyone?

CHAPTER FORTY-ONE

Autumn

I can hear in his voice that he's not happy when I call.

Obviously, the reunion upset him, but I didn't expect it to last this long. I'm the one who should be upset. He left me there without even saying goodbye.

Had she not been there, we would have been finally moving forward. We were hand-in-hand walking into a crowd of people. He kissed me and put his arm around me. It wasn't a secret anymore. But when he turned and walked away without saying a word, then hasn't talked to me since, it feels like we're back to square one.

Actually, I think we're farther back than square one. More like in the negative zone. After everyone found out and all the drama ensued, we've spent less time together than when it was a secret.

I've tried to face it. I've tried to listen to Kory when she *'pointed out all the facts.'* I've tried to prepare for the worst, like my mom said. But I can't give up. Not when we're so close.

While it was true that we seem to be getting nowhere, I'm ready to fight for it. I need to spend time with him. We need to spend time *together*.

"How are you?" I ask.

"I'm okay. What about you?"

"I'm good. I have an idea, actually."

"What's that?" he asks.

"Let's go away this weekend. I rented a Lakehouse. Let's get out of here and away from all the hotels, people, and drama. Just us." He doesn't say anything. My voice saddens. "I just want to spend time with you, away from it all. This has been a lot for me, too, and I just need to get away for the weekend. I really want us to spend it together. I don't want to go without you."

He finally talks. "I don't think I can this weekend."

My heart sinks. "Why not?"

"Just not good timing. I think I have something going on with my brother."

I'm quiet for a minute. "I just thought you'd want to get away from it all. From all the noise. Do you remember the Lakehouse?"

I feel like I hear a faint smile in his voice when he responds. "I do. And I would. I just can't this weekend."

I accept the rejection. "Okay then. See you soon though?" I ask.

"Yeah, soon."

"Okay then. Soon." I repeat, not knowing what else to say.

This isn't how our conversations go, and just like that, it's over.

Kory came with me, although it wasn't what I wanted. I tried to be hopeful he would change his mind. A whole weekend, just us, was all I wanted. Time for us to just talk and *'figure it out' together*.

I thought the sentiment would win him over. December wasn't the time of year most people would go to a Lakehouse, but it was special to us. At least I thought it was, but once again, maybe it was just special for me.

I know he loves me now, or he wouldn't have just willingly been at a public event with me. They'd all heard about it, but now they've seen it. That's why we needed time alone. Time away from everyone's judgmental comments and uninvited opinions.

If I had a dollar for every time I've heard that what we have isn't real, I'd be able to be on vacation for the next two years. But I know it's real. It always has been, and he's finally on the same page, so I don't want to give up.

At least that's how I felt before we got here yesterday. But already in this short time away, I've started to figure out that we are really still right where we have always been, just with more complications. He's had so many chances, both then to say that he wanted to be with me, but he didn't.

And now we're doing it all over again.

Even though she wasn't the guest I intended to have, Kory is still the greatest best friend I could ask for. She is being so supportive and doing everything I need her to do without me asking. She's always been great at that, though, knowing the right thing to do at the right time.

She's been here to just listen and talk, but has also given me the perfect amount of space. If I wanted to go out on the town and keep myself busy, she was down. If I wanted to lie on the couch with a blanket and a sad movie so I could blame my tears on that, she was down for that, too. Even though we talked about going out and I knew she wanted me to, I just couldn't do it. I was a mess.

While the couch and a movie sounded great, I spent most of the weekend in one spot. The very same spot I'm sitting in right now.

The Lakehouse has a reading nook up in the loft. It is a small, cushioned spot that sits right against a big bay window looking out on the water. The tall panes give a clear view of the tranquil scene; the seemingly unending water, slowly lapping on an empty beach.

There is hardly ever anyone on the beach in the cold. Not even the seagulls. But the water hasn't frozen, so it's the one thing in view that's moving, all by itself, back and forth, over and over again. I stare at it, hoping it will put me in a trance.

But it doesn't. Sitting here is actually doing the opposite for my brain. It's such a beautiful view of the lake, and so close to where I did the morning after prom; instead of hypnotizing me, it's just become my favorite place to cry.

The stairs start creaking underneath Kory's feet as she climbs them, coming to check on me again. Her steps keep getting closer until the light from the lamp is blocked by her standing in front of it. But I don't turn to face her. I don't wipe my cheeks or pull the side of my head off the cold window. I don't move at all.

"Hey," she says quietly as she sits down next to me.

I don't respond, and she doesn't push me either. She just joins me at my silent showing of the lake.

"How cold do you think the water is?" I finally ask.

"Uhm, probably freezing considering we're supposed to get snow tonight." I nod my head in quiet agreement. "You thinking about going for a swim?"

"I don't really know what I'm thinking right now," I whisper.

"You wanna talk about it?"

"I don't even think there's anything to talk about at this point."

She blows frustrated air through her lips. "Of course there is. It may not change anything, but there's plenty to talk about."

"I don't know, K," I finally cave. "I don't know anything. What am I even doing?"

"Right now? You're wallowing and taking time for yourself, which personally I don't think is such a bad thing as long as you plan on returning to being a normal functioning adult before we leave."

I shoot her an irritated look because, for the first time, this is not the time. She's got me talking, but wants to be funny. I'm not in the mood for her funny.

"Fine," she concedes. "Just tell me what's been going through your mind up here, and I'll be quiet and listen."

"I just don't understand what is so hard for him. It was so easy and so good, then he just changed overnight. I don't understand how a feeling supposedly so strong can be one-sided. He can't possibly feel the same way I do, or I wouldn't be sitting here with you, no offense."

"None taken." She throws both hands up.

"I've never felt not good enough before for anything. I mean, I guess I did a little bit back then, but I also never made much of an effort to try *us* then. This feels…" I pause to sniff the snot that is trying to escape my nostrils. "This feels like garbage, like I'm nothing to him, when he's everything to me."

She scoots closer to me and sets her hand on my leg. "Hey, hey." Her voice is calm and comforting. "You are not garbage, and you are not nothing. Don't ever think that about yourself. Ever." I wipe my cheek. "I know how bad you wanted this, and honestly, I wanted it for you, too, because I know what he's always meant to you. But Autumn, a relationship that makes you feel this way is not a relationship worth being in."

I don't argue with her. I can't argue with her. She's right.

With nothing else to say, I just lean my head into her. She wraps her arms around me, pulling me in tight. "I love you, Autumn, but I hate this for you." She says as I allow violent sobs to fall into her chest.

I want to fight for him so badly it feels like it's killing me. I keep begging my heart to let it go and to give up, but it just keeps telling me to scream at him. To somehow beat it into his head that we've come this far, so we can't stop now.

But despite my will to fight, I feel my heart finally losing. Something else inside is starting to scream at me instead, drowning out my heart's voice.

Screaming that no matter what he said to me all summer, no matter what I did, no matter how much or how long I've loved him, no matter how much I know he loves me, he is never going to be mine.

CHAPTER FORTY-TWO

Jimmy

I've never fought for anyone before, and I think that's why I feel so lost, why I've felt so lost this whole time.

I don't mean to be cocky, but I guess I was just lucky. The girls I liked always liked me back. Most of the time, I was the one to end things, and if I wasn't, it didn't really bother me when they left. If they left, it usually had to do with Autumn. They never had an actual reason, though. Becca does.

I know it's my fault. This whole thing is my fault. What is even the first step in fixing it? Admitting I did it? *Did that.* Saying I'm sorry? *Did that.* Saying I'm sorry over and over again? *Did that too.* So now what?

Flowers are out of the question. She's never liked flowers to begin with. I bought them for her once, and she tried to be nice, but I could see it all over her face.

Honestly, she's always been hard to do anything romantic for because she doesn't like any of those things. Even after all these years, she's hard to shop for because she doesn't like surprises. She likes order. She likes things to be the way that she thinks they're supposed to be, with as little nonsense as possible in the way. That includes gifts, because if I surprise her with something she doesn't specifically want, it's a waste of our money. I gave up trying to surprise her a long time ago.

But I'm out of options, so even though she hates surprises, and she told me not to, I'm here outside a bar. I had to see her on her birthday. I need to show her in any way possible that I really will do anything, and it wasn't hard to figure out where she'd be. I still know Izzy, and Izzy still knows everything about everyone, whether we like it or not.

With sweaty hands, I walk inside. I see her right away, with four or five girls who look vaguely familiar. It's Becca that I hardly recognize.

She's dressed in a way I've never seen before. Her jeans are tight, cradling her hips. She has a gold top on that's definitely new, and as she turns around, I see the middle of the shirt drops down loosely, damn near to her belly button. I don't know who this person is, because I'm having a hard time believing it's my wife.

Her friends notice me before she does, and they obviously know who I am. I watch them whisper to her, and she looks up. I smile. She frowns.

"What are you doing here?" she asks as she stomps towards me. Her high heels click across the floor, something else she doesn't normally wear.

"I told you I wanted to come." I smile again, hoping she will too, but she still doesn't.

"And I told you I was doing this without you."

The heels she's wearing bring her closer to my eye level than I think I've ever seen her before. Now I can see that she also has on new makeup. The dark colors covering her eyelids, coupled with the thick eyelashes, bring out the color of her eyes. Her lipstick is bright red. A color she's never worn before. I've only ever seen that color on one other person. *No, not right now.*

I reach for her hand. "Come on, Bec, please. Can we have just one conversation? Please?"

She looks back at her friends, then pulls her hand away. "Fine. One conversation and that's it. Outside."

She grabs a jacket, a thin black one, not at all suitable for this weather, and walks towards the door. I follow. We sit down on the empty patio furniture. No one is out here because it's December and freezing. I know she doesn't plan to talk to me for long. I stare at her until finally asking,

"So how have you been?"

She glares at me. "Really? That's what we're going to do right now?"

I shake my head. "No, you're right. I'll get right to it. I've already said I'm sorry, but I'll keep saying it. I'll keep saying it forever until you accept it. I'll do this as long as I have to. I know I have no right to, but seeing you with someone else..."

Her laugh cuts me off. "Yeah, I saw you staring. Staring while you were standing next to *HER*. We're here because *you* were with someone else, remember?"

I knew that was coming. "I know. I said I have no right, but I'm telling you the truth, and I needed to see you. I needed you to see me say that I'm sorry. Not just hear it through the phone."

"You sound ridiculous, Jimmy. I'm not your problem anymore. You don't get to be offended that I was with someone else. It's actually just making me angrier. You should go."

"No, please, listen." I plead. "I'm not saying I'm angry. I'm not. I'm just saying… seeing you with someone else… made me realize how much I miss you."

She looks away before speaking again. "How many times are we supposed to do this, Jimmy? I believe you didn't sleep with anyone before, but really, it's all the same to me. How many times are we supposed to walk this tightrope of '*are we actually okay or not?*'"

I ignore the fact that these past fights she keeps referring to were baseless and all brought up by her insecurities. I just sit here and continue groveling, because I know that's what she really wants.

"I know. I know. There aren't enough ways I can say I'm sorry. There aren't even enough words to describe how sorry I am. For all of it. Everything. I didn't realize it then, but I was stupid, and I do now. Being without you, I see it all."

She shakes her head. "I told you the last time was the last time. And that was nothing compared to this."

"This is the last time. I promise you. We will never be in this situation again."

She sits quietly for a minute, rubbing her shoes around on the cement. Her friends are at the door, scowling at us. She sees them and stands up. "I'm going back inside to finish celebrating my birthday with my friends. We'll talk more next week?"

I jump up. It's not a yes, but it's not another no. "Yes. Whatever you want."

We hug for the first time in months.

"I'll call you when I'm ready."

"Happy birthday, Becca. I love you so much."

She finally smiles and nods, then walks back to her friends. I stay on the bench for a while, with a smile on my face, ignoring the cold.

We're going to make it. I know Becca, and if she's decided to talk to me, she's decided it's going to be okay. *We* are going to be okay.

I just hope I am.

CHAPTER FORTY-THREE

Autumn

To make the weekend at the Lakehouse worse, I didn't hear from him at all. Not one time, and I just couldn't take it anymore.

As soon as I wake up in my bed, I call him again. It's early on a Monday, but I am done waiting for responses. We are either happening or we aren't, and today is the day he is going to give me an answer, whether I like it or not.

He answers, but once again, doesn't sound like his once-happy self—someone who is excited to hear from me. I get straight to the point.

"Can I see you?" He doesn't respond right away. "Please?" I whisper.

"Are you home?" is all he says.

"Yes," I reply just as short.

"Give me two hours," then he hangs up.

The quickness of the conversation fires up that gut feeling, but he's coming here, which is better than a parking lot, so I ignore the alarms. But then he texts me when he gets here, instead of walking right in. I text him back, telling him to come up, and a few moments later, he joins me on the couch.

I don't bring up the reunion. He's finally here, and I don't want to push him away again. But I don't know what *to* bring up. Why are we like this? What happened to the easiest friendship I've ever had? Why are we struggling with small talk?

"How was your weekend?" I ask. Asking it sounds as weird as it feels.

"Not quite as exciting as I hoped," he says. He adjusts himself, and his hand lightly brushes my thigh.

The small talk is too painfully awkward, so I just reach up and give him a kiss. I don't know what I expect, but he kisses me back, and it's like a flame hits gasoline. I jump up and straddle his lap. His hands grasp my hips, then they're in my shirt, and I feel their warmth on my back. I've missed these goosebumps.

I grab his shirt and lift it up over his head. He grabs mine and pulls it off next. His fingers are tangled in my hair while his lips press against my neck. I reach down to the button of his pants. Just as I get them undone, he grabs both of my hands.

"Stop. I can't."

I freeze, panting. "What?"

He leans his head back, resting it on the couch, and covers his face with his hands. "I mean, I can't do this anymore, Autumn."

I am still frozen. Lost and staring at him while he stares blankly at the ceiling. I get up and snatch my shirt off the couch.

"What is happening right now, Jimmy?" I demand, temporarily controlling the crack in my voice.

He leans forward, putting his head in his hands. "I'm sorry."

I throw the shirt at him, realizing I grabbed his anyway. "YOU'RE SORRY?" He doesn't say anything while I start losing control. "For what? What are you actually sorry for? That it's not a secret anymore? That it's not fun for you anymore? Or are you actually sorry for lying to me this whole time?"

He's still sitting calmly. "I'm sorry for all of it."

His emotionless demeanor sets me off even more. "If you're so sorry, then why are you even here? Why did you come here? And why did you just kiss me?"

He finally stands up and faces me. "I'm here because you deserve to hear what I have to say face to face, not over the phone."

I feel like I can't breathe. Every breath fills my lungs with fire. My heart is beating in the most painful way. A way that I've never felt before. It feels like it is going to pound right through my chest. Each beat vibrates through my whole body. I fold my arms tightly across myself, as if that will protect me from what's about to happen; what my gut has been trying to warn me of for weeks now.

"Hear what?" I whisper. My voice finally cracks.

He runs both hands through his hair. "That I want to make things work with my wife."

I take a deep breath, closing my eyes and biting my lip. "This is about the reunion, isn't it? Does she even want to be with you?"

He looks down at the floor. "This isn't about the reunion. It's about my wife and what she deserves."

My spiraling begins. In fact, I spiral more than I've ever spiraled before. I throw my hands up in the air and involuntarily do a 360-degree turn.

"What *she* deserves? And what about me, huh? What do I deserve? I know I am not an angel in this situation, but did I deserve for you to come and ruin my life? To screw my whole world up and turn me into something I'm not?"

"Of course not," he says quietly.

"But screw me, right?" I yell. "Now you can go be the good guy. You can go make things right with her and convince everyone you've learned your lesson and can be the perfect husband. And then there's me. I'll always be the bad guy because I was the other woman. The stupid, stupid other woman. Getting away from you was the smartest thing I ever did. I should've stayed gone."

He finally makes eye contact, and I see surprise in his eyes. *Had he really not known that?*

"Yeah. Because apparently, I was smarter then than I am now. I loved you..." I stop for a second and take a jagged breath, but it hurts even more. I can already feel the scars from the fire in my lungs. "SO much..."

Saying it out loud crushes me, and the tears are now uncontrollable. My lips tremble as I finish. "I loved you SO much, Jimmy. But you. You would never admit that you loved me back. And I knew you were never going to, so I left. To save myself. To save myself from you breaking my heart just by being you."

I laugh sarcastically and wipe my cheek. "And look at me now. All I did was prolong the process. I thought ten years later, and you being married, everything would be fine, and maybe I could even have my best friend back, but no. Because you're still… *You.*"

I watch him stare at me while I pour my heart out, and it clicks that I am still just in my bra, so I grab my shirt and put it on. Once I pull it past my eyes, I see him coming closer, trying to hug me.

"NO!" I jump back and grit my teeth. "Don't you dare."

Now that he's closer, I can't avoid looking directly at his eyes. They are as red and wet as mine. I don't think I've ever seen him look like this.

"I didn't know that's why you left." He whispers and reaches for me again.

"I said DON'T. Get away from me. You don't get to cry to me now because you were too dumb to figure it out all this time. Why are you even crying? YOU did this. You made this choice. Go home and do it. Maybe it is your turn. I'm done after today. I can't even look at you anymore. Go crawl back to your wife and cry to her."

"Don't say it like that." His voice cracks, and he sniffles.

"I'll say it however I damn well want to. Because you know what I deserve? I deserve to react however I want to. You deserve NOTHING from me. Or her, for that matter. I actually hope she tells you to go to hell. I hope you get to wallow in this mess you've made all alone and live with what you've done to all three of us. It doesn't feel good to cry, does it? But this is exactly what you deserve. To feel just like we have. To live with the fact that you ruined your closest friend in the process of it all."

He continues to stare. I see an actual tear on his cheek, but something has finally changed, and I don't care. The amount of anger piercing through me is overflowing, and continuing to ramble ten years of erased messages feels like a pressure release valve has been opened.

"And you know? I hope that bothers you most of all. All those times you joked about hating the guys I dated. All those times you cheered me up when some asshole did something stupid, or all the times you told me they didn't deserve me? When all along it was YOU who didn't deserve me."

"Can I say something?" he whispers.

"I don't care to be honest. Say whatever you want. It doesn't matter anymore." I roll my eyes.

"You're right, you didn't deserve any of this. Just know that I'll never regret anything, except for right now. I don't regret being with you, affair or not. And your friendship has meant the most to me out of anyone in my entire life."

I shake my head and wipe my nose. "Yeah, I supposedly meant the most to you, yet you destroyed me. And you'll miss me. You're going to miss me so deep into your core that each time you think of me, I hope it kills you a little bit. I hope you miss me like I'm dead. Because guess what? I am. That old me that you remember and *'love so much?'* You killed her. And you're dead to me, too. I never want to see you again."

He stares at me. I grab his shirt and throw it at him again. "Go on." He continues to stare as he pulls it over his head. Then just sits there and stares some more. I re-fold my arms. "Well? Go."

He stands up and walks toward the door. I can't look at him anymore. I don't want to watch him leave. I feel my face swelling back up, so I turn in the other direction. I stare out the window and wait for him to be gone, but just as I hear the door open, he stops.

"Autumn." He says with a shaky voice. My name on his lips feels like needles in my skin now. "It's the right thing to do."

I close my eyes. "The right thing to do, or what you actually want?" He doesn't respond, and I wish I hadn't just asked that question. Hot lava pours down both my cheeks. "Get out, Jimmy."

It's silent for a minute. "So this is it?" he asks.

I breathe in and reply as I exhale, "This is it. Don't ever talk to me again."

Ten excruciating seconds pass until I hear the door click shut. At the very same instant, I fall onto the couch and turn into a salty puddle that smells just like my favorite cologne.

CHAPTER FORTY-FOUR

Jimmy

A week passes with no call from Becca.

No calls from Autumn either, although I didn't really expect one. I anticipated it being bad, but the hatred I felt from her, the look in her eyes, was indescribable. I thought Becca's face bothered me, but Autumn's? Autumn's was something entirely different. Autumn's will haunt me. Was it possible I hurt her more than my wife?

Everything she said to me was right. I didn't deserve her. Then or now. I didn't deserve to ever even know her if this was what I was going to do to her. I know I got used to her absence before, but when she left then, it wasn't the end of a friendship. It felt abrupt and confusing, but it never felt like the end. This was different. This was *the end*.

And like she said, I have to live with that. She was also right when she said it would hurt like death. I have to mourn the death of the greatest, longest friendship I've ever known, and the fact that there is no way she can ever be in my life again. I have to mourn, and I have to move on.

I know Becca said she'd call, but I couldn't wait for her anymore. I have to know I made the right choice. I drive to our house, hoping her schedule hasn't changed in the few months I've been gone. Thankfully, as I pull in the driveway, her car is there. So I sit in mine, trying to prepare what I'm going to say. Nothing sounds right, so I just go.

Knocking on my door feels so foreign, but I do it anyway, and to my surprise, she answers right away.

"Hey," I say.

"What are you doing here?" she asks, but friendlier than last time.

"I don't know really. But you haven't called yet, and I had to try something."

"Why didn't you call?"

"I don't know. Because I've already tried that? And I want to show you that I'll try anything. I needed to see you, and the more I thought about it, the more I realized I just needed to be here. Please don't make me add this to my list of regrets."

I smile nervously and, shockingly, so does she.

"Okay, come in."

An even stranger feeling than knocking on my door is feeling like a stranger in my own home. I follow her to the kitchen like I don't know where I'm going. Rex flies down the hallway and nearly takes me to the floor. I missed him, too. Becca grabs two waters out of the fridge and hands me one. We sit down across from each other at the island, the spot where we've always sat and talked the most.

"So do you have a speech prepared?" she asks, "I saw you practicing in the car."

She smiles. I smile. We're getting somewhere.

"No, I don't. I don't know what else to say, but I needed to do something. I didn't even know if you'd let me in, but I had to show you I'm still trying. So I'm here, trying. Anything and Everything."

"Well, I told you we could talk."

I nod. "And I appreciate that."

"But I have some things to say, too. If we're going to move forward, you're going to tell me the whole truth, answer every one of my questions, even if you think I don't want to hear it."

"Anything you want," I tell her.

CHAPTER FORTY-FIVE

Becca

Just like I knew he'd call after the reunion, I also had a feeling he'd just show up at some point if I kept avoiding him.

I told him *'next week'* just to give me time to get my thoughts together, and I'm honestly surprised he waited the whole time.

I knew deep down that if he still wanted to be married, I would stay and work it out. But I needed him to be gone to make that choice. I want him to choose me because he *wants* me, not out of legal obligation. The reunion date may have been a petty push, but I could've done worse.

But now he is here, and if we are going to do this, I want everything on the table, even if it hurts. I know I told him that first night, I didn't want to hear him admit any of it, but I can't move on with him with secrets still hanging above our heads. And I won't look stupid again, so I need to know everything.

"Anything you want." He says.

I take another drink of water and begin my interrogation. No more avoiding anything. "Did you guys ever actually date in high school?"

He looks at me like I'm crazy, and maybe I am, but as I said, I'm done wondering about anything that relates to the two of them.

"No?" he answers with question in his voice.

"But you guys had to have been sleeping together?"

"We did, but only twice. Not like everyone assumed."

I nod my head, both surprised and somewhat pleased with that answer. I was right, but I was also one of those people who assumed way more than twice.

"Did you talk to her while she was gone?"

He immediately shakes his head. "No. I truly had not spoken to her since she moved. I didn't even know she was moving back until she was practically already here."

"Practically?"

"Yes. I heard rumors she was moving back, but I didn't even really think they were true."

I nod. "Did you message her first?"

He put his head down. "Yes." He looks back up. "But I didn't mean for this to happen. I just wanted to catch up with an old friend. We had lunch and that was it."

"But then you obviously kept talking?"

He nods again. I wait for him to say something else, but he doesn't, so I continue instead.

"When was the first time you slept with her? This time around." He rests his head in his hands. "You said you would answer," I insist.

"When you were gone for graduation."

I nod. That's what I suspected once I started putting pieces together. "I'm just going to assume that this wasn't a one-time thing?" He looks back down at the floor and shakes his head no. "So you found a way to keep sleeping with her? How many times?"

"I don't know."

That stings a bit, but I asked for it. "Did you ever bring her here?" My voice drops, fearing the answer.

"No," he says adamantly.

"When was the last time you slept together?"

"A little while ago." He says right away. "I swear. I just couldn't deal with anything or anyone. I was so confused, I just started avoiding her. I don't remember, honestly."

"So, it wasn't just after your little date to the reunion?"

He shakes his head. "No, I left her there."

A giggle slips out. I knew that, but just wanted to hear him say it. But then I get right back to business. "Sorry, okay, when was the last time you saw her?"

He looks me straight in the eye. "Three days ago." I tilt my head to the side, and he continues. "But it was to end it. I hadn't seen her since the reunion. If you want me to be honest, I knew I was going to hurt her, too, so I was still avoiding her and the conversation." I stand and listen since I have a feeling there is more. "She kissed me. Or I kissed her. I don't remember, but we kissed, then I stopped her and told her it was over, and I wanted my wife."

I was going to ask who broke it off. "Yeah, and how'd that go?"

He looks at me, confused. "Not well. But it's done. We haven't talked since, and even if I wanted to, I'm positive she wouldn't."

"Even if you wanted to?" I questioned.

"I didn't mean it like that. Not saying I want to. I'm just saying, I know it hurt her. She hates me and rightfully so. Rightfully so for both of you."

"Did you tell her you were going to leave me for her?"

"I may have given her that impression."

That's not an answer to me. "Did you or did you not, Jimmy?"

"Okay. Yes. I did. I'm sorry."

"I can see why she hates you." I sit and ponder for a minute. "Do you love her?" He stares at me. "Answer the question, Jimmy."

He takes a deep breath. "Yes, I do, or I did. I don't know. It's not the same as being in love with you. It was my past, and I shouldn't have let the two mix together. I know I am in love with you. I want this. I want my wife. I want our life."

I sit on that for a minute. I already knew he loved her, and I appreciate him not lying to me about it. "Well, lucky for you," I start, "Even though I keep trying, I can't hate you. So now what do we do?"

He shrugs, "I don't know. I was hoping you would tell me."

I tap my fingers on the counter, then begin the speech that I had prepared and practiced. "What you did was NOT okay, and I'm telling you right now that I don't know for sure I can get past it, but I can try. I know you two have a long history. I honestly couldn't believe how lucky I got when she left, and then you asked me to go to that party with you." I take a breath. "And I know that history means feelings for each other. This summer made that clear, and those won't just go away, no matter how bad I want them to. I also know you love me. But most importantly, I know that I am not her and I never will be. If I am who you want to be with, we can do this. I've never seen myself with anyone else. I never even had a picture of my future until we started painting it together."

I pause, watching him listen.

"But we're too old to not know what we want. I want you, but I only want you here if you truly want to be here. Your family is my family, and I love them. I don't want that to change. Whether I like it or not, I know there's a little piece of your heart that's always been hers and probably always will be. But if you can leave that piece in the past this time and I can have the rest of it from here on out, that's enough for me."

He walks around the island to be closer to me and grabs my hands. "That is *everything* I want. I married you to be with you. I'm so sorry that I let it get like this. But I promise this is what I want. Right here, right now."

I let my guard down for the first time since August and lean into his chest. He wraps his arms around me, and suddenly the air in this house feels a million pounds lighter.

We're going to be okay.

JUNE 2020

CHAPTER FORTY-SIX

Autumn

One summer. It took one summer to ruin my life.

I allowed my life to become such a disaster in such a short time. I was a mess, and I could really only be mad at myself.

As much as I blamed it all on him at first, it wasn't all his fault. I allowed it to happen. I was a willing participant in something that hurt so many people, including myself.

And the worst part about it was that I was *so* happy. I was so hopeful that this was it for us that I ignored every gut feeling telling me it was wrong and that the end was certain. The more I dwelled on it, the more I convinced myself that I deserved this, too.

I deserved to spend months alone and miserable. I told him he would have to live with it, not yet ready to accept that, so would I. I would also have to live with my part in the mess. So, I did.

I moved on, living life alone again. I worked and I slept. I occasionally caught up with Kory, but in reality, the *'catch-ups'* were her coming to check on me. The more she told me she was worried about me, the more I wanted to crawl into a hole. I was worried about myself, too.

You know that scene in New Moon after Edward leaves and Bella sits in the window for months? That's exactly what those first few months felt like for me. The holidays and even my birthday passed in a hopeless blur.

I did nothing. I was in a depressed, robotic-like routine, and it was rare that I left my bed. Unlike Bella, I had to pay bills, but if I wasn't at work, that's where you'd find me. Crying was my only hobby. I don't know if I slept or cried more, but I definitely preferred sleeping. I didn't feel anything when I was asleep.

I knew this would happen. At eighteen, I knew leaving him where we stood was my only choice. I knew it. But I came back anyway, and I think *that's* actually the worst part.

Before I knew it, the sadness was gone, and only anger was left. I was mad at myself. I was mad at him. I was mad at Becca. It wasn't her fault, but I couldn't help it. If he'd never been with her, we could've been so happy, so good together.

But that made me mad at myself again because had I never left, would they have even gotten together?

I thought getting out was the answer, but maybe my leaving was what, in fact, ruined our chances. Had I not run away, maybe everything would be different. I was also mad that I didn't try to call him again. Why did I only try once?

And then I was mad at him again. Why didn't he try harder to talk to me when I left? Why didn't he fight for me then? Why couldn't he just admit his feelings, and I would've never left in the first place? If he had asked me to stay, I would have. But he didn't. He didn't even text me back.

Not that I wanted to be seen out in public anyway, but I couldn't bring myself to leave my apartment because I didn't want to see him. I couldn't. It was a risk I knew I couldn't handle.

My mom would bring me groceries, not so subtly checking up on me, too. She would sit at the foot of my bed, quietly rubbing my leg. I knew she didn't know what to say, but she wanted to be there, and I appreciated that.

I had to block both Jimmy and Becca on social media, too. Avoiding them in person wouldn't help if I could see them through the phone screen. I was never friends with Becca, but I could see her posts if he was tagged. She posted a picture of the two of them, cuddled up on the couch with Rex and Rosie *the cat that didn't like him*, clearly all happy to have him home. I couldn't stand the thought of seeing their updates as they moved on with their wonderful life, while I couldn't get out of bed.

As tears flowed, I wished they could turn into a river to transport me back to my apartment in Wisconsin, back to a time when at least I was happy being alone.

But then in March everything changed again, for the worse, even though I didn't think that was possible. *The COVID-19 pandemic.*

I no longer had time to reel in my self-pity. My work life had also suddenly been rocked to the core, and people were dying around me every day.

In this line of work, we try to mentally prepare for the loss of patients because you know it's going to happen at some point. But nothing prepares you for something of this magnitude.

No amount of schooling prepares you to hold the phone while family members cry and say their goodbyes via video chat.

No textbook prepares you for the number of phone calls you have to make, telling people their loved one didn't or won't make it.

No medical research prepares you for your hospital to run out of equipment, and there is literally nothing you can do for new patients until someone else dies.

Then, on top of it all, worrying about your safety.

The world stopped. Schools closed, stores closed, even doctors' offices closed. Places that were open only allowed a certain number of people in at a time and made sure everyone stood six feet apart. People were even sanitizing their groceries after they bought them.

But we couldn't close. We were the one place that had to remain open and couldn't even guarantee that *'safe'* distance because we had beds everywhere. People who were coming in for regular things weren't receiving the care they needed because hospitals were overloaded with COVID patients. Routine procedures were cancelled or pushed far out into the future. Some nurses like me were pulled from our departments to help with the increase in need in the ERs and ICUs.

Once COVID hit, my life, which was already flipped upside down, got picked up and shaken, emptying out everything I had left.

At some point in the chaos, hospitals started searching for travel nurses because the demand never slowed. Medical staff were quitting, and some got sick themselves. Other regions were hit harder than us, and they just needed more people. Hospitals literally ran out of staff, so they were paying people to relocate and work for them for a contracted amount of time. As soon as I heard about the opportunity, I took it.

Yes, I was absolutely running away again. But I needed that break. I wasn't just running away from him and the looks I still received every now and then; I was running away from that hospital, which had become another source of trauma.

I knew I wasn't going to save everybody from COVID, but by getting on that first plane, taking the chance to get out of there and away from everyone we knew, *and an immense amount of virtual therapy*, I saved myself.

CHAPTER FORTY-SEVEN

Becca

Did I expect everything to go back to normal as soon as he came home? No.

But did I expect to feel like we were walking on eggshells for as long as I did? Also no. It was awkward for a while. Maybe I shouldn't have asked all those questions that night. I thought I wanted to know everything, but then I wished I didn't. It took some time not to think about her every time I looked at him. To not wonder if it was her when his phone made a noise.

We never talked about it. I told him I wouldn't bring it up, so I didn't, but I couldn't stop thinking about it.

For a while, it felt like it did before he left. He barely talked, and I wondered if there was even a point to us trying to be together again. I asked him once why we were even back together, and it blew up. We didn't talk for three days. I'm sure it didn't help that we weren't sleeping together like a married couple should. You know, making time to be husband and wife, like his mom would awkwardly bring up sometimes. Did I think that was counterproductive to moving past an affair? Maybe, but I couldn't bring myself to do it. Whenever I thought about having sex with him, I thought of her, of them together. I definitely couldn't initiate it. Part of me hoped he would, even though I didn't know how I'd respond. I still wanted him to try.

I didn't know how we were going to make this work, but everyone knew he was back, so we were going to make it happen.

When COVID hit, both of our jobs basically stopped. Once we were quarantined together, we had no choice but to finally confront it head-on. The weirdness between us. There was entirely too much time in the house together for us to avoid each other anymore.

Natural conversation started slowly but eventually returned to normal, well, like two years ago normal. The more time we spent doing everyday tasks like cooking, cleaning, learning how to place online grocery orders, and binging TV shows together, the better we got.

It wasn't until I started feeling the baby steps towards a better place that I finally felt a tinge of guilt for the first time. Guilt for not telling him *my* whole truth. I told him no more secrets, yet still hung on to one of my own. I thought about telling him, but knew it may change his mind. Wrong or not, I couldn't let that happen. We were going to come out stronger from this. Even though I did finally feel a little guilty about being the one with a secret, I still stood by the fact that I did what was best for us. And I was still doing that by not telling him. Plus, my secret was nothing compared to what he did to me, so I was content with living with my omitted truth.

It took a good three or four months from quarantine to actually get to the place that felt *good* again. And I knew we officially made it when we finally slept together. It had been just over ten months, which doesn't sound like a lot, but felt like forever.

It was midday, during a Netflix session, when he just leaned over on the couch and kissed me in a way that I had forgotten. We didn't even leave the couch. It was after that when I finally felt like a husband and wife again. I chose to ignore the voice in my head pointing out that Autumn had just once again left town.

The timing was just a coincidence.

AUGUST 2023

CHAPTER FORTY-EIGHT

Jimmy

My mom was officially declared cancer-free a week before COVID took over the world. We had no idea how lucky we were with that timing.

No one was traveling, and the hotels were desolate. I'd never seen anything like it. People had to be laid off, even though we hoped that at some point we'd just have to rehire all those positions. Schools first shut down, then all went virtual. We were supposed to *'Stay Home & Stay Safe,'* so Becca and I spent almost all of our time at home together for a year and a half. Watching the world become virtual was surreal. It still sometimes feels like a fever dream.

The first couple of months of my being back home were hard. I could tell she didn't trust me, and to be honest, I didn't trust myself. I struggled with the whole thing. I wanted to be with my wife, but I struggled to get Autumn out of my head. I think she could tell, too, because it was rough.

The timing of quarantine was a blessing in disguise for us. I know for a fact we wouldn't be where we are today if we hadn't been given that time alone with little distractions to do nothing but talk and work through the things that needed to be worked through.

The unending quality time also brought us our biggest blessing yet. On May 20th, 2021, Becca had our baby girl, Emery.

After having adjusted to teaching virtually, some colleges opted to keep virtual classes as an option. Becca chose that route even after schools opened back up. She was able to be home all day with the baby, then teach classes virtually in the afternoons and evenings when I came home.

Three long years later, everything is basically back to normal. The seriousness of COVID has subsided, and everybody is back to living *'normal'* lives and doing *'normal'* things. My work went back to normal rather quickly. When people got the opportunity to travel again, they jumped on it.

Another positive that came out of COVID was Will and Chelsey moving back closer to home. They were also obviously enjoying quarantine and welcomed my niece Allison, just three months before Emery. We couldn't believe our luck and wanted to enjoy every minute of it.

Chelsey and Becca were trying to enjoy their first pregnancies together, and we wanted to enjoy the little ones growing up close. I know he had a hard time leaving, but they were back by the time we found out we were both having girls. What a celebration that was. Especially for our mom, who had raised two boys.

It took some time, but everything fell together for everyone.

And then, as we're all settled and happy again, fate has to insert herself in the most torturous way.

Every Thursday, Will and I take the kids to the park while the wives get some time together. I had a work call to make this morning, so he offered to take the girls to play, giving me a few minutes to handle it. I just finished the call, and I look up to see her standing on the other side of the pond.

She changed her hair. It's shorter, sitting just past her shoulders. The wavy curls bounce while she walks, and as she turns, I notice for the first time since I've known her, she doesn't have bangs. It opens up her face more, and besides the new hair, she *still* looks the same.

I knew it was Autumn before I even saw her face. The way she walked. The way the sun painted her hair gold. She was alone, walking along the path that circles the pond between us. The same path we walked together just a few years ago. It is good to see her, to see that she is, on the face of it, doing okay.

I snack on some peanuts and think about it all. How different things were four years ago and all that's happened since. I haven't seen or heard from her since that day at her apartment. One of my least favorite days in existence, besides finding out my mom was sick. She did a good job avoiding me at first, then once again, she was a ghost. I couldn't help but wonder where she went, and if she'd come back again.

I knew I made the right choice with Becca, but it took a while to get over how I made Autumn feel. I wondered and hoped that it didn't take her as long as it did me to be okay and to be happy again.

I see her now, and the feeling is both the same and different. It makes me smile, but not just in the way it did before. I'm relieved to see that she looks good. Happy to see her smile at two bunnies as they roll around with each other, then dash into the bushes. But also, I find myself still longing to hear the laugh that I love.

Part of me would like to say hello, to ask and know for sure that she's okay, but I won't.

As much as it hurts, I know enough now to know that the past needs to stay right where it lies, and for us, that's in 2019.

CHAPTER FORTY-NINE

Autumn

I see him sitting there.

I can't tell if he saw me, too, but that is my luck. A short visit home, and I see him on the first day, again.

I can't help but keep looking at him as I come around the path. I probably shouldn't, but I tell myself I'll say hello if he's still sitting there once I make my way to the other side. It would be more awkward to just look at each other as I walk by and not say anything at all, right? Just pretend like we don't know each other. *Right?*

I turn away from the pond and pause for a minute, letting the August sun tattoo my skin. I can't just walk by him and act like I don't know him. I never could.

Once I make it over there, he's still in the same spot staring at his phone. As I get closer, he looks up and smiles. I approach him with a quick, awkward hug.

"Hi," I say.

"Hi," he says back.

"How are you?"

"Doing really good, actually. You?" He asks.

"Good. I'm good too."

We both smile. I didn't know what I was going to say to him at first, but since we're here and alone, I'm going to get something off my chest.

"I'm glad I ran into you. I just want to say I'm really sorry for all that stuff I said to you. For the whole thing. You really don't deserve to be unhappy forever, and it wasn't all your fault. I hope none of that stuff I wished on you actually happened." We both laugh awkwardly.

"No, it's okay. I understand. I'm sorry too. You didn't deserve any of that either. I'm happy to hear you're doing good."

A high-pitched voice breaks the uncomfortable silence that follows. "Daddy!"

A small child runs past me, brushing up against my leg. It's a little girl with blonde pigtails, and coming up slowly behind her is Jimmy's brother holding another little girl about the same size.

"Hey sugar," Jimmy says in such a small, sweet voice. A voice I've never heard him use before.

My eyes are wide with both shock and delight. I can't believe what I'm seeing. He leans down to pick her up. "Did you have fun at the playground?"

"Yes. I went down the slide fifty-eleven times."

He laughs, then looks at me, "This is Emery. Say hi, Emery." The little girl waves.

"Nice to meet you, Emery," I say.

She holds up all five fingers on her hand. "I two now." Jimmy and I both laugh.

"Well, well, well, I recognize that voice," Will says as he leans in for a hug. "Back again so soon?"

I laugh. "No, actually not at all. Just visiting for my dad's birthday. Trying to visit them more this go around."

"Well, it's good to see you." He says.

"You too," I respond.

I look at Jimmy laughing and tickling his little girl. My heart swells. He looks so happy. And I genuinely feel happy for him. Fatherhood looks good on him. Will breaks the silence again, probably noticing I'm staring.

"So, you still living the high life, traveling all around?"

I shake my head. "No, actually, I stopped traveling. I uh, met someone in one of the cities I was working in and decided to stay there for a while. We'll see what happens."

Out of the corner of my eye, I see that Jimmy looks up at me, then at his brother.

"Nice." Will continues. "So where are you at now?"

"In New Jersey. It's nice. I like it there. This is the first time he's been out of the state, so it's kind of fun to feel like a tourist in my own hometown." We all laugh.

"Oh, he's here? What's up with that? You hiding him from your old friends?" he antagonizes.

I laugh. "No, he's actually in a Zoom meeting for a couple of hours back at my mom's. I just decided to get out and enjoy some fresh air. We're only here until Sunday morning."

"Brought him back to meet the parents, huh? Must be serious." He winks.

"Yeah. Actually, I think it might be." I shyly smile and see Jimmy do the same. I quickly change the subject to make my way out of here. "Well, I don't want to keep you guys." I say, "It was so good to see you both, though."

They both say you, too, and I share a quick hug with each of them. I wave to Emery and the other little girl, then we all take our leave. They go the way I came from, and I continue walking the path I was following. I turn back to look just one last time.

Jimmy is chasing Emery, and when he catches her, he effortlessly swings her up in his arms. They spin in a circle, and he sees me looking.

We share one last goodbye smile before turning back in our opposite directions.

CHAPTER FIFTY

Jimmy

Neither of us talks for a few minutes.

We walk in thick silence, watching Em and Allie scamper around, picking at grass and late-season dandelions and searching for butterflies.

I listen to the splashes from the fountain. I inhale the smell of fresh-cut grass nearby. I feel the roughness of the denim as I rub my sweaty hands on my jeans. I focus on the bright colors of the flowers throughout the greenery. Anything to keep me grounded.

I only looked back twice, and she only saw me the first time. I know her smile meant goodbye, and as much as it hurt, I was so glad this one went differently from the last.

We make it to the other side of the pond, where the girls get distracted by the vast number of dandelions in one patch. They run into them, and we sit down at a bench to let them explore. I focus on my daughter but struggle not to picture Autumn out there playing with her.

I often wonder where Emery got her blonde hair from. Genetics is a funny thing, and I'm convinced that the ones she got are just fate's cruel way of constantly reminding me of someone else.

"How're you doing?" Will finally asks.

I don't even plan to play dumb. I'm sure he's been wanting to ask me questions for years. When Becca and I got back together, no one in the family asked questions, including Will. We all just moved on, leaving it all behind us. I've never told him the full truth about how I've felt since, and I'm still not sure if I can do it now.

"I'm okay," I say.

He looks at me, waiting for me to say more, but I stay quiet. "Are you sure?" he prods.

"What do you mean? I'm good." I know I sound frustrated. I am, but not at him. Frustrated at myself because I'm losing it. He notices my agitation and laughs.

"Whatever you say."

The girls are still frolicking, so I follow up with another question. "What do you want me to say?"

"You don't have to say anything. We just haven't talked about it. I figured after that you might want to."

I sigh. He's right. I do kind of want to. I've wanted to get it off my chest. I just didn't expect anyone to understand. But at the same time, if anyone would be willing to try, it's him.

"I still think about her all the time. I never stopped."

He nods like that's what he was expecting me to say. "What do you think about?"

"Everything," I confess. "I wonder what life would be like if any one of us had made *one* different decision. Especially me." He listens. "Like what would it look like if I chose Autumn. Where would we be right now? Or what would've happened if Becca told me to go to hell? I'm sure in that moment I would've run back to Autumn, who probably would've slapped me in the face." He laughs. I keep going. "I also wondered what it would've been like if Autumn were a different type of person. One that wouldn't have respected my choice. Would she have kept fighting for me? Made mine and Becca's life a living hell?"

"I wondered all those things at first, too." He confesses. "I started working on my speech to Chels, convincing her that Autumn is not the devil, and they'd probably love each other."

That makes me laugh. Allie falls, and we both brace ourselves for tears, but she gets up and all is well. "I think a lot about that conversation we had at your house. I was so sure then that it was Autumn. It wasn't until I was already back home that I started trying to figure out what changed, why I changed my mind so fiercely, because I missed her so much."

He puts his head down like he's finally disappointed in something I've confessed. I probably should shut up, but now that I've started unpacking all of this, I can't stop.

"I know. That makes me sound like a real asshole, but it's the truth. Once I was back home, the differences between the two were front and center like never before. Yes, things would've been different for me and Autumn, but I know it would have been good. I missed her free spirit, her always-happy personality. I still do. I always felt the most like myself when I was with her."

"I don't think you're an asshole." He starts. "I think it's good that you're finally being honest with yourself."

Emery laughs. Allie squished the dandelions in her hand, and they discovered the yellow stain it leaves behind. Now they're picking them just to squish them.

"I don't regret my daughter," I say boldly. "And I don't regret being married to Becca. But I do regret not giving me and Autumn a real shot."

I know that makes no sense. But I don't try to defend it. He doesn't question it either. "Did you try and talk to her at all after you went back home?"

I shake my head. "No. I knew better than that. I did try to look her up, just to see how she was doing. I was a mess, and I was hoping she wasn't. Or maybe I hoped she was as messed up as me, I don't know. But then, when I did, I realized she blocked me altogether. That hurt."

"What are you going to do now?"

"Nothing. Whether I like it or not, it's over. Even if Becca were to up and leave me one day, there's no turning back. Plus, she's happy with someone now…"

My thoughts trail off. I'm happy that she's happy, but that feeling in my stomach is back. She's with someone and said it's serious. The thought bothers me. I want to know about him. I feel protective and irritated that I'm still blocked, so I can't know anything about who he is, even though I have no right to anyway.

"Are you going to tell Becca you saw her today?"

I laugh. "Are you kidding? No. We ran into her mom one time, and she had an attitude for the rest of the day because I talked to her for *'too long.'*"

"Great, so now I have to lie to my wife too?" he asks.

I look at him, hoping he's joking. Thankfully, he follows it with a laugh. "I'm kidding. I got you on this one, but promise me you won't get me mixed up in anything worse."

I nod my head, and we're quiet for a minute while I zone out on the dandelions. I picture her here again. I know she'd be out there, down in the grass, having just as much fun as the kids, not worried about getting her clothes dirty. It makes me smile.

Emery looks at me, holding her handful of dandelions up like a trophy. I still see Autumn, clapping proudly behind her. *How can I look at my whole world and still wonder if things could've been different?*

I do miss the fun I had with Autumn. I know it wasn't just the affair because we always had that much fun. I know we still would as *'grown adults.'* Why couldn't we? Aren't you supposed to enjoy life with your partner? She was my best friend, and no one else has ever come close. No one has come close to making me feel the way I feel about myself when I'm with her.

But that's all gone. And just as she said those years before, I have to live with the fact that I'll never even *know* my best friend again.

And just as I feared, now that I've seen her again, I'm struggling with the thought of that.

"You didn't lock that door like I told you to, huh?" he finally asks in a low voice I barely hear.

"I can't when she has the key."

Giggling interrupts as my little girl runs up to me, hands in the air, covered in a mess of tortured dandelion petals.

CHAPTER FIFTY-ONE

Autumn

I get back to my mom's and make myself a drink.

Tyler is still in his meeting, and my mom is taking a nap, so I sit on the porch by myself. I think about the morning and realize that I've never felt so content. I smile as I take a sip and picture Jimmy's smile with his daughter. He seemed so effortlessly a dad. I could see his joy when he looked at her, and for some reason, it meant so much to me.

The awkwardness that I expected when I mentioned Tyler only lasted for a quick second. He smiled, and I could see in his eyes that he was happy for me. I was more thankful for that than I expected.

I could also see a familiar look on his face. The look that led me to believe he had questions he wouldn't ask. And even though he didn't ask them, and we didn't say much, I feel like today finally gave us the closure we needed and the ending we both *actually* deserve. I am happy and I *am* doing good.

I sit and continue to think about it all. That summer was a whirlwind, and thankfully, I can finally look back on it now with happier feelings. We were so lost in the *'what could've been'* story that we got swept away in it. I know I did. In my mind, we were almost there, right at the finish line, and that was enough for me. I lived for every chance I got with him and didn't care about anything else. I didn't need anything else other than him. I loved him more than I loved myself, even though he was never even mine.

But then seeing him today as a dad, I know there was and is so much more to life than the feelings we had as teenagers.

While enjoying the sunlight, I hear the door open. Tyler comes out onto the porch and gives me a kiss. I stare at him and revel in the peace I feel from this exact moment; the closure from my past, and the happiness that comes from the person sitting next to me now. I look over at his tan skin, nearly shimmering in the light. He looks at me and smiles; I see a sparkle in his blue eyes. I've never met anyone with his caramel complexion and such light-colored eyes, but I could literally stare into them for hours. Just looking at him makes me happy, and just being near him makes me feel safe.

We met about a year and a half ago, coincidentally, at a park. One thing I learned in therapy was to get back to finding happiness with myself. Loving myself again and being okay being alone. I took that advice and started regularly going to the park to walk whenever the weather was nice. No matter where I was living, I could find a park somewhere, and that's exactly why I was there today.

I had been in Jersey for about two months. He approached me once and asked for my number, but I politely declined. But then I saw him again. I didn't pay attention to his eyes the first time, but they won me over that second time.

We talked for a couple of weeks, then eventually went on a date, and another, and then another. We only dated for a couple of weeks before making the relationship official. Then we only made it five months before he told me he loved me. The whole thing moved fast, but I was more than ready to be happy and loved again.

Giving him a chance was perfect timing, too, because I had already started thinking about leaving the travel nursing behind. I really liked Jersey, so the search for a local job was already happening before the thought of a relationship.

A little over a year later, here we are at my mom's house, where earlier he had asked me to move in with him when we got back. That's another reason I was at the park: to clear my head and think about taking that next step. He smiles, and I realize I am still looking at him.

"What are you thinking?" he asks. "You're staring at me. It's getting creepy."

I smile. "Just thinking. About you. I'm happy you came here with me."

He smiles back and steals my cup for a drink. "Me too."

"Also," I started. "I think it's a good idea."

"What's that?" He hands me back the cup, and I take a drink. "Moving in with you."

He grins ear to ear. "Great, because I already told your mom you were when we got back. Also, Kory's coming back with us to help."

I stare at him with a surprised smile. In moments like these, I realize that I'm still not used to some of the smallest things. Telling people. Going behind my back to plan something.

I was so committed to doing whatever it took to be with Jimmy, secrecy became ingrained too deeply in my brain. Just the thought of being back here, in this town, sitting on this porch, visibly in love, makes my heart swell more.

I have no words. We both laugh as he stands up and comes closer, grabs my hands, and lifts me up to stand. He wraps his arms around my waist, and I throw mine around his broad shoulders. We hug each other tightly.

"I love you a lot, you know that?" he says into my hair.

I hug him tighter. "I know. I love you so much, too."

Still enjoying his arms around me, I see a familiar red car drive past the house. It slows near the driveway like it's going to stop, but then continues down the street. The shape of the car seat in the back seat confirms why it looks familiar.

I watch the car shrink in the distance, and for some reason, my smile grows. I don't know why he came here, but I know it doesn't matter anymore.

Tyler's arms are still loving me tightly, standing in the same spot that Jimmy and I stood in fourteen years ago, saying goodbye.

The same spot where I cried, hoping he would say the one thing I wanted him to, the one thing that could've changed everything, but he didn't.

The same spot where, as a grown woman, I cried in my mom's arms over him still not loving me three years ago.

The same spot that used to hold so much pain and sadness.

Today I'm in that same spot, with someone who is ready to shout on the rooftops how much he loves me and how happy he is that I'm moving into his house.

It's the moment I know that I am finally right where I'm supposed to be.

"Hey Siri, play Daylight by Taylor Swift."

EPILOGUE

Autumn - Two Days Later

Kory's arm is linked with mine as I drag her through Newark Liberty International Airport.

"So, these are the air trains you have to get on to get to each part of the airport." I point to the map on the wall.

"This looks like what I envision a space center would look like." She says, analyzing the diagram.

"I know, crazy, right? Confused the shit out of me when I first came here."

Still attached, I pull her in the direction we need to go, almost completely forgetting that Tyler is right behind us, pulling our bags. I glance back at him, to which he smiles, and I turn back around, resting my head on her shoulder.

"Thank you for coming," I say into her ear.

She scoffs. "Are you kidding? Thank *you*. I've never needed a break from Scottville more than I do now."

"Well, that's not hard when you've literally never left. Except to visit me wherever I am."

We both laugh. "Exactly, and look where that's gotten me?"

Her playful jab refers to the fact that she is habitually single; no relationship has ever really gotten serious. She claims this most recent one was, but also seems to have made it out of the break-up completely unscathed, so I can't imagine how serious she really was. It was just a couple of weeks ago, and I expected to play her role of the supportive, comforting best friend during this visit, but she barely even mentioned him. Actually, she hasn't mentioned him at all. I brought him up, and she shrugged her shoulders like it was nothing.

Oftentimes, I do really feel bad because she is the best when it comes to my ever-revolving door of relationship drama. One of these days, I hope she does actually let me return the favor. However, I find that unlikely anytime soon because aside from our physical distance, she hardly lets anyone close enough to do any real damage. In that sense, I envy her.

Once Tyler drops us off at my apartment, she immediately drops her stuff on the floor.

"So, where do we start?"

I know she's referring to packing up my stuff, but instead, we spend the next two hours doing absolutely nothing but talking and draining a bottle of wine.

The next morning, Tyler shows up as promised, at 9 a.m. sharp, with coffee and way too many boxes. Thankfully, thanks to my two years of traveling, I don't really have much, and I warned him of such, but he's the *'better safe than sorry'* type.

Hours of packing and splitting a large pizza on my empty living room floor—everything I own is in boxes—once again. It's sobering for a moment that I always seem to end up here. But then Tyler's blue eyes catch mine, and suddenly the boxes don't matter anymore. I throw my arms around his wide shoulders and give him a kiss.

"I'll start loading the truck." He says with a smile.

"Thanks, babe," I say as he starts stacking boxes and lifting three at a time like they weigh nothing.

When the door clicks shut, Kory starts talking while taping a box labeled "Kitchen." "So you think this is finally it for you?"

Her statement catches me off guard a bit, causing a nervous laugh to bubble out of me. "Well, yeah, I think so. Obviously. Why?"

She shrugs. "I don't know. I just want you to be like really sure, ya know?"

I look at her through tight eyes. Maybe she has the right to question my decision-making when it comes to relationships, but why start asking me these questions now? When everything is already packed?

"This isn't a rebound, Kory. Jimmy was three years ago. I'm good, I swear."

Before she can respond, Tyler saunters back inside, once again effortlessly stacking four boxes and swooping them up in his arms.

"Is that what you're worried about?" I resume once the coast is clear. She doesn't respond—distracted by her phone. She's obviously reading something interesting as I watch a smirk crawl across her lips.

"Hello?" I snap my fingers. She immediately returns her face to neutral and fumbles to put her phone back in her pocket. "That who I think it is?"

She shakes her head, but doesn't look up at me, obviously about to bullshit me. "I don't know, but it was just Olivia."

It's definitely bullshit, but I don't say anything as Tyler walks back in the room again.

It's a long three days, but at this point, Tyler's house is officially mine too. My shoes sit by his at the front door. My toothbrush sits in the stand next to his. My favorite coffee mugs hang on his hooks. My clothes are in his closet, and the pictures that used to hang on my wall are now sitting on his TV stand. *This is it.*

Kory didn't bring up her obvious apprehension again, but it's lingered on my mind. And it wasn't until about five minutes ago, as I was making note of all of these things, that the question finally crossed my mind. *Is this too fast?* My judgment may have always been clouded by infatuation before, but as I watch him, once again dragging all of Kory's bags behind him like a golf caddy, I know this isn't that. He loves me and I love him. For real this time.

What also hasn't left my mind—Kory's constant distraction by her phone. Even now, while we're at the airport about to send her back home, her eyes roll at the screen—the way they do when she flirts—before she quickly types something and returns her phone to her pocket.

"What's Liv up to?"

"Oh, not her that time. Just El being stupid."

Elliot? Her brother? I struggle to stifle my laugh. I believe that less than I believed the other day was Olivia. Before I can call her out, the call comes through the speakers for her to board her flight.

"I love you." She says and squeezes me into a hug.

"I love you too." I squeeze her right back, savoring this moment—to last me until we see each other again. "Text me when you land."

"I will. Thanks, Tyler." She waves toward him before finally turning away.

I watch her walk, dark brown tendrils of hair bouncing with each step, intrigue settling heavy in my stomach. Part of me hopes that her phone will slip out of her pocket and I'll be able to beat her to it, so I can find out who she's been talking to. The chances of that scenario playing out are slim to none, but God, I wish I had her phone in my hand. I'm probably going to have to visit soon because this is going to gnaw away at me. For the first time in twenty years, my best friend is flat-out lying to me.

I didn't push her this time, but next time I see her—I will find out everything. The smirk gave her away. It wasn't the one she wears when she talks to her brother or one of our old friends. It wasn't just amusement. It was something else. Something she hoped I wouldn't see. Whoever is the cause of that smirk clearly makes her feel something, which means she'll pretend they don't. The worst part of her being so secretive, though? I'm pretty sure I already know exactly who she's talking to.

Even though we've shared everything—every secret, every fear—one of Kory's greatest/worst skills has always been building walls. Walls, she doesn't let anyone break through. Sometimes, like now, that even includes me. If I'm right… If it is him… then these walls are either to protect my feelings, or to protect hers in order to protect mine. Kory is the type of best friend who would choose our friendship over her own happiness.

What she doesn't see is that if she'd ever finally break those walls down completely, she'd know she doesn't have to choose. She might tell you that those were built to protect me, but they're not. They've always been there to protect herself.

I just hope she doesn't take too long to finally realize it.

STORY INSPIRATION SOUNDTRACK

Seven—Taylor Swift

The Last Great American Dynasty—Taylor Swift

Mad Woman—Taylor Swift

Hoax—Taylor Swift

Illicit Affairs—Taylor Swift

Invisible String—Taylor Swift

Mirrorball—Taylor Swift

Betty—Taylor Swift

Cardigan—Taylor Swift

The Lakes—Taylor Swift

Exile—Taylor Swift (feat. Bon Iver)

My Tears Ricochet—Taylor Swift

This is Me Trying—Taylor Swift

Peace—Taylor Swift

Epiphany—Taylor Swift

The 1—Taylor Swift

August—Taylor Swift

BOOK CLUB/DISCUSSION QUESTIONS

1. In the first 5 chapters, we glimpse each of the main characters' personalities and varying views of the past. Do you think the differences in personalities are the sole reason for the contrasting views of their younger years?
2. After living alone for 10 years, Autumn is seemingly a confident, independent woman. However, upon returning home, it doesn't take long for her life to revolve around Jimmy. What are your thoughts on that change?
3. Jimmy wonders if Becca is insecure because she is jealous or jealous because she's insecure. What are your thoughts on this? How may her past play a part?
4. Autumn struggles with her identity as the "other woman." Do you believe being a mistress automatically makes one a bad person? Or can a really good person make a really bad choice?
5. Between Jimmy and Autumn's memories, we get a clear view of what happened on the night of Autumn's prom. They both hung on to the memories from that night, but with very different feelings. Why do you think that is?
6. With a past like Jimmy and Autumn's, family inevitably gets involved. What do you think of their responses to the situation? (Autumn's parents. Jimmy's mom and brother.)
7. Jimmy's attitude changes significantly after the affair becomes public. Why do you think this is his initial reaction?

8. Discuss the reunion. Each character goes through a range of emotions during that short time period. What were your reactions to that night?
9. Were you surprised Becca chose to forgive Jimmy? Discuss your thoughts on why she changed her mind.
10. Think of the title, *Scars of August*. How do you think this title connects to the story? To each character?
11. Lying, or omitting the truth, has been common among all 3 of them throughout their lives. Discuss which lies each of them told and how the truth could've changed things.
12. Concerning their lies, how many of them were lies they told each other or lies they told themselves?
13. Another common theme throughout the story is friendship. Both Jimmy and Autumn touch on the fact that, despite how much it meant to them, their friendship will likely never recover. They both allude to that loss being the tougher heartbreak. Discuss your thoughts on that.
14. Jimmy & Becca both share the awkwardness that existed when they got back together. Discuss your thoughts on this? What do you see for their future?
15. In the last scenes, Autumn and Jimmy run into each other after another couple of years apart. Discuss their interaction. Think about where Autumn and Jimmy were in regard to their friendship/relationship at the beginning of the story, versus where they are now.

ACKNOWLEDGEMENTS (SERIES EDITION)

The biggest 'thank you' is to the readers who made Scars of August as successful as it is! I appreciate every single one of you. We wouldn't be here with a "Series Edition" and book two on the way if it weren't for you!

To my street team, thank you for all the hype, support, and the funniest secret conversations. Being an independent author is like having five full-time jobs, and you all make it just a little bit more fun.

To the narrators of Scars of August, Emily and Jason, thank you for loving the original version and doing such an incredible job capturing their personalities as well as the emotions each one displayed. Emily, I am especially impressed by your ability to voice two characters—giving them each their unique voice. I'm not sure if there is anything better than hearing your story performed back to you.

To my editor, Elaine, you are a superhero. Truly, I don't know why I thought it was ever a good idea to publish this without you, but thankfully, I came to my senses. Not only do I appreciate your knowledge, but the commentary made my whole night some nights and literally had me laughing out loud.

To my cover designer and interior formatter, K. Jaspersen, thank you for making it look as beautiful as I imagined it could be. Your talent and eye for detail are incredible!

To my character artist, Delilah Monroe, thank you for taking the images from my head and turning them into real-ish people. LOL It's a surreal feeling to see something that is so important to you become something tangible.

To my husband (again) and best friend. Thank you for joining me—physically—on this journey. From toting heavy boxes, pulling wagons full of more heavy boxes, going to get me drinks because my table is so busy, to just listening to me babble about everything that has happened in the last six months. All of the in-person events I got to participate in since Scars of August's release couldn't have happened without you.

And once again for good measure, the readers. THANK YOU. I wouldn't have the team of people to list of above if it wasn't for you all. I honestly still can't get over the fact that I just typed out all of those people. I'll never be able to say thank you enough.

ACKNOWLEDGEMENTS (FIRST EDITION)

First, I thank God for giving me the talent of putting ideas that start in my head onto paper. For giving me the passion I've always had for reading and writing, and the ability to multitask my way to a finished product

I thank Sean, my husband, for his unending support. His willingness to listen and nod while I ramble on about parts of the writing/publishing process as I'm excited about them, even if he doesn't really get why I'm so excited. I appreciate the way he gives me space and doesn't bother me when he sees I'm sucked into a trance on my laptop, even though it means I may be there for hours. I love that he encourages me and helps me come up with new ideas to get my book out there to the public. Thank you for all of that, plus so much more. I love you.

A big thank you to Taylor Swift. Yeah, I am aware of how incredibly cheesy that is. But the inspiration for this story came from her Folklore album, my favorite album of hers. The music and her storytelling on that album inspired this idea, and the more I ran with it, the more excited I got about the possibilities. I had so much fun writing this, and I imagine that connecting the pieces of this story felt similar to how she feels when she puts the pieces of a song together. Musical artists put music out that they love and feel passionate about, just hoping we'll feel the same. That's exactly how I feel about this book. So yes, thank you, Taylor, for your music and inspiration.

To my online Swiftie friend Elizabeth, whom I still haven't even met in person. Thank you for posting in that group and catching my attention with our shared love for folklore and storytelling. I appreciate you looking at this project in its infancy and loving it so much that you made me love it even more.

My sisters. While I know you would support just about anything I do, thank you for your support throughout this process. Thank you for reading each draft as it developed and telling me when my ideas hit the way I wanted them to, and when they didn't. I can't wait for you to have this physical copy, because there's still stuff in this final version that even you didn't see coming.

Lastly, my cousin Autumn. Thank you for letting me use your English major to fine-tune the details of this project. Oh yeah, and your name.

ABOUT THE AUTHOR

Ashley Pierce lives in Southeast Michigan, where she was born and raised. A lifelong fan of psychological thrillers and romances, she brings real-life Michigan moments into her fiction, blending hometown charm with emotional depth and suspense.

She writes a wide range of stories—some gripping and intense, others heartfelt and romantic—giving readers something fresh and unexpected with every book. She prefers handwriting her stories— with a pen dripped in experience, emotion, and hometown pride.

Ashley spends her non-writing time reading and spending time with her husband, kids, and dogs, usually outdoors or at the lake.

THANK YOU FOR READING!

Please visit my social media to keep up with all new announcements and events!